CAT SEBASTIAN

The Missing Page

Page and Sommers Book 2

First edition

This book was professionally typeset on Reedsy.
Find out more at reedsy.com

Acknowledgement

This book wouldn't exist without the enthusiasm of those readers who asked for another book in the Page & Sommers universe and then patiently waited for nearly three years while this project was repeatedly derailed by illness, pandemic, moving, misbehaving computers, sick pets, and a parade of inconveniences both large and small.

This book owes a tremendous debt to Rose Lerner's book doctoring. After approximately seven billion revisions there was still something seriously amiss, and Rose was able to zero in on what wasn't working. It was like sending a book to therapy.

In addition, I'm grateful for Kim Runciman's copyediting and to Bran at Crowglass Designs for the beautiful cover.

Content Notes

This book contains references to period-typical queerphobia; queerphobic family members; discussion of suicide, including the suicide of a parent; and manipulative/undermining behavior by a psychiatrist.

CHAPTER ONE

C ornwall, February 1947

When James descended from the platform of an unfamiliar train station and climbed into a waiting taxi, he was already in an unspeakable mood, raw and vulnerable as an undressed wound.

Perhaps he could blame the weather, which was as gray and damp as any February could hope to be. Perhaps it was because he had just spent four hours on a train with no amusement other than a book that revealed itself to be a sorry disappointment mere minutes into the trip. Perhaps it was because somebody had left a newspaper on an empty seat, and all it took was a single glance at the front page to confirm that it contained nothing but tales of danger and strife. Danger and strife, in addition to being generally unpleasant, now held the added complication of being all too likely to occur in places where Leo was sent.

Leo would be back in England by the beginning of March. James held that thought carefully, just out of view, as if it might dissolve under closer scrutiny, and therefore his mood remained as bleak as the relentless monochrome of the landscape.

When the taxi pulled up in front of Blackthorn, James was fully prepared to hate the sight of the place. It had survived in his memories as something of an enchanted castle, but childhood memories were notoriously unreliable, and James knew himself to be lamentably prone to bouts of gauzy nostalgia. Blackthorn was likely nothing more than a mid-Victorian monstrosity, crusted over with all manner of turrets and whatnot.

But the house that stood before him mapped surprisingly well onto the Blackthorn of his memories. Admittedly, there were turrets and crenellations and more towers than one would think a relatively modest country house could accommodate, but the more egregious excesses were softened by a good deal of ivy and something James didn't think he could quantify. Charm, perhaps.

He frowned, vaguely irritated not to find the house tasteless. There really was no pleasing him today, was there? He paid the cabbie and wrapped his muffler a second time around his neck to ward off the cold wind that blew in from an unseen sea.

Suitcase in hand, he stood on the gravel drive, gritted his teeth, and turned in a circle. There was the apple tree Rose had taught him to climb; there, in the distance, were the stables where Rose had shown him a litter of kittens. And, of course, at the bottom of the garden was the path that led to the sea. As a child he hadn't properly understood the gravity of the situation. But as an adult—indeed, as an adult some years older than Rose had been that final summer—he had the sense that he had stumbled across a hidden graveyard. It made him want to turn around and get the first train back to Wychcomb St. Mary.

But he had come for a reason. Well, that wasn't quite true—he had come because there was no reason not to, and James, for good or for ill, wasn't in the habit of denying requests. The old man had been good enough to remember James in his will, and if he had seen fit to require the presence of all his legatees at Blackthorn, then it would be churlish and ungrateful for James to decline. And if James privately thought it quite odd that Uncle Rupert—solemn, dour, rather a killjoy—would go in for such a set piece as gathering the family for a reading of the will, then he could keep that to himself for a day or two.

He knocked on the door.

At the back of his mind he had expected the door to be answered by the butler, or at the very least a housemaid. The Blackthorn of his memories existed in a time before butlers as a species had practically gone extinct.

Instead, the door was opened by a small woman closer to fifty than forty, with pale hair that was more gray than blond, a tea towel clutched in one hand, and a face James was startled to find familiar even after twenty years. "That can't be Jamie," she said. "Or, bless me, I suppose I ought to call you Dr. Sommers."

"You ought to do no such thing," James said warmly, putting down his suitcase and holding out his hand. "Cousin Martha, it must be." It was funny, now that he thought about it, that Rose and Camilla had been plain Rose and Camilla, but Martha was always Cousin Martha. She was only a few years Rose and Camilla's senior, but that had been enough to firmly establish her as a proper grown-up, even if her poverty hadn't already set her apart from the daughters of the house. All that nuance had been lost on him as a child, but it was embarrassingly clear now, as he took in Martha's worn tweed skirt and moth-eaten

4

cardigan.

He realized that he hadn't any idea whether Martha had ever left Blackthorn. Was she as much a guest as he was? Or had she stayed here for the past twenty years, still keeping house for Uncle Rupert?

"I'll show you to your room and then you can make yourself at home," Martha offered, reaching for his case.

"I have it," he said easily, his hand closing around the handle.

"Of course you do," she said, looking at him oddly. "You were always such a sweet child." There was something almost wistful in her expression, something he might have classified as regret, if that made any sense at all.

Not knowing how to respond to that, as he could hardly accept a compliment bestowed on a version of himself that was twenty years out of date, he pasted on a smile. "Am I the first to arrive?" he asked, curious as to who else had been summoned to this gathering.

"Mr. Trevelyan is in the library," Martha said as they climbed the stairs. "Did you ever meet him when you stayed here? Oh, well. I daresay young boys don't take much notice of elderly solicitors. We're still waiting for Camilla."

"Is that all?" James had thought that if Uncle Rupert's will included as distant a relation as James, it must also name a number of other beneficiaries.

"Mr. Trevelyan asked me to prepare five bedrooms. Those two at the end of the hall will be for Camilla and Anthony. They've always used that pair of rooms." She paused in front of a closed door. "And this room is yours. I haven't any idea who the other two rooms are for. Now," she said, opening the door, "I think you'll find everything you need. I'd tell you to ring if you want anything, but there isn't anybody to ring for these days. You'll have to try your best to track me down, I'm afraid."

And that, James supposed, answered his question about whether Martha was not only living at Blackthorn, but still serving as an unofficial housekeeper. James assured her that he wouldn't need anything and leaned against the closed bedroom door.

He hadn't thought Sir Anthony Marchand would also be at Blackthorn. He had rather counted on the man not coming, in fact. Surely, Sir Anthony had patients in London and better things to do than attend the will reading of his late father-in-law. Surely, he had a full schedule of being smug and officious, and couldn't possibly spare the time for a trip to the country. With any luck, the remaining empty bedrooms would be occupied by people with sufficient neuroses and obsessions to keep Sir Anthony busy and far away from James.

James told himself not to be unkind. Sir Anthony had done his best by James, all things considered. Hadn't he?

He started unpacking his suitcase, then crossed to the window and peered out. The view wasn't what he expected. In fact, he hadn't been aware that he expected anything at all until he saw nothing but brown and gray.

What he had expected—what he remembered, in some part of his mind he hadn't been aware even existed—was an expanse of green leading to tennis courts and then to the sea. The green of high summer was of course absent from this February landscape, and the tennis courts were overgrown and barely visible. And there Rose crept into his mind once again, the memory of her laughingly berating someone for a bad serve as James ran around the court, collecting stray balls.

As suddenly as the memory appeared, it drifted away. Still,

he knew that if he opened the window and stuck his head out, he'd catch a glimpse of the sea. It was funny, the things one's memory saw fit to throw at one out of nowhere. He hadn't thought about the view from Blackthorn since he was a child, and now he could vividly remember throwing the window open to see the merest fragment of the ocean.

Not that he would do that now. It was cold and damp outside and only marginally less cold and damp inside. He cast a doleful eye on the empty grate. There was neither electric fire nor radiator anywhere in sight.

Well, at least he had brought plenty of warm clothes with him. He had grossly overpacked, not knowing whether this was to be the sort of weekend where one dressed for dinner. Was it to be a jumper and corduroy trousers sort of weekend or a tweed jacket and tie sort of weekend? As the only invitation he received had come not from a hostess but from a firm of solicitors, there hadn't been anyone to ask. He already felt peculiar about returning to Blackthorn after so long and for some reason was loath to do so in the wrong clothes. As a result, James's suitcase was close to bursting at the seams despite the fact that he planned only to stay a single night. The letter from the solicitor's firm indicated that he was welcome to stay from today—Friday—through the entire weekend, but Leo might return any day now. And since Leo's stays in England tended to be measured in days rather than weeks, James didn't want to waste an hour of whatever time they had.

The thought was oddly jarring, thinking of Leo as he was standing in a house he had occupied as a boy. Maybe it was because the idea of Leo was so out of keeping with memories of carefree summers and endless sunshine. Or maybe it was because James was now living a life his twelve-year-old self couldn't have imagined and didn't even know how to hope for.

Or maybe it was just that he had never quite believed Leo would return, and being so far from home made it seem that much less likely that Leo would ever find his way back to him.

He groaned at his own capacity for hand-wringing. This was what came of time off work, he supposed. He abandoned his suitcase and went downstairs.

CHAPTER TWO

L eo dug his fingers into the coarse fabric of his seat and shut his eyes as the airplane flew through a pocket of rough air over the Channel. Less than an hour and he'd be on British soil. A few hours after that and he'd be in Wychcomb St. Mary.

That was what he needed to think about: a warm cup of tea and whatever tin of soup James decided to heat up. He needed to think about going to sleep with James by his side and knowing that when he woke up, James would still be there. He could spend all of tomorrow in the pair of James's pajamas that Leo had claimed as his own, watching James grumble over the cryptic crossword as they drank milky tea. There would be nobody shooting anybody else and certainly no question of whether Leo thought they ought to be doing so.

And there his thoughts went, skittering away from Wychcomb St. Mary and into the usual swamp.

Leo was used to jobs going sideways. During the war, he had been reasonably pleased with himself if half his missions yielded anything close to success, and even those tended to end with somebody trying to shoot him.

By any standards Leo was familiar with, this job had been an

9

unqualified success. He had done what he was sent to do and nobody had shot him, not even once. He had even managed to wrap things up days ahead of schedule. He ought to feel good about it, all things considered.

So what if there were two more dead bodies somewhere in Vienna. One had unquestionably been a Soviet spy, the other an American agent, and Leo hadn't killed either of them. But the spy had been barely more than a kid, and Leo didn't like it.

Kids got caught up in this business all the time. Nobody paid them much attention and they were good at lying and brilliant at holding their lives cheap: they made natural spies. That was how Leo had started out himself.

But during the war it had been easy to cultivate a flexible understanding of good and evil. And even when that flexibility was stretched to the utmost, Leo trusted his handler. That trust had turned out to be a bad idea, as trust usually was, but it had smoothed over a lot of things his sad excuse for a conscience might otherwise have got tripped up on.

Now Leo didn't have his old handler and he didn't have a war. And he didn't have any good reason why that kid and that American weren't breathing anymore. Was a strategically placed radio worth it? Leo didn't know and he was vaguely embarrassed to even care. He ought to have got over this sort of silliness years ago.

For the hundredth time in the past couple of months, he decided that he needed to get out of this business. He was no good at being a peacetime spy; this entire line of thought was proof enough of that. But Vienna had been his third mission since Christmas, his third mission since his handler retired and Leo found himself absorbed into MI6. His third mission since James had given Leo the spare key to his house and space in his wardrobe. Every time he told himself it would be his last mission.

And he also told James it would be the last. He never meant for it to be a lie, but somehow even Leo's attempts at honesty twisted their way into untruth. James deserved better. Christ, Leo was beginning to think that *he* deserved better too, and wasn't that an alarming thought.

When the plane landed, Leo couldn't scramble down the stairs fast enough. He ought to go in for a debriefing, but that could wait until Monday, protocol be damned. Instead, he hired a car to take him all the way to Wychcomb St. Mary. It was a frightful expense, but he thought that if he had to wait a single minute pacing the platform at Paddington, he would work himself into a frenzy.

When the car pulled up in front of James's house, though, all the windows were dark and there were no signs of life inside, despite this being Friday, a day James ordinarily had clinic. He paid the driver and knocked on the door anyway, but nobody answered. Leo's own key hung on a hook inside; he could hardly have taken it to Vienna. He considered picking the lock, but the odds of getting something good to eat were much higher at Little Briars than they were in James's kitchen, so to Little Briars he went.

Edith Pickering answered the door and gave Leo a disapproving once-over that Leo was beginning to suspect signaled concern. "James isn't here," she said by way of greeting.

"I figured he was out seeing a patient," Leo said, handing Edith his coat. It was the same coat he had put on early that morning in Vienna, with a spot of blood still on the cuff, and seeing it in Edith's clean hands made him want to snatch it away.

11

"I wish he were doing anything so sensible," Edith said briskly, leading the way into the sitting room. "James has gone to Cornwall." She said this as if announcing that James had taken up a life of crime and perversion. "Some uncle of his died and he's gone for the reading of the will."

Leo bent to kiss Cora Delacourt on the cheek. She looked smaller and frailer every time he saw her, even though her mind was still sharp when she wanted it to be. "I didn't know James had any relations," Leo said, "let alone one who would leave him anything."

"James was surprised as well," Edith said. "The letter from the solicitor said the uncle's will stipulated that all legatees attend the reading at the family home in Cornwall or forfeit their bequest."

Leo's eyebrows shot straight up. "Was it his uncle's dying wish to reenact a radio drama?"

"That is precisely what I asked," Edith said, handing Leo a cup of tea, "but James said his uncle had been entirely sane and not at all given to theatrics."

"Quite right," said Cora from the sofa. "James's uncle was Rupert Bellamy. You remember him, Edith. He was a few years older than us. He could make no conversation unless it was about golf, tennis, or banking. I shouldn't have said he had a fanciful bone in his body, but I haven't seen him since 1910 and I daresay people change." She spoke these last words with a heavy dose of skepticism that Leo wholeheartedly shared.

The more Leo thought about it, the less he liked it. Leo had read this detective story and he had seen the film and knew that when you made the heirs gather together, they immediately started putting exotic poisons into one another's tea. They simply couldn't help themselves.

Leo had been awake for over thirty hours and was aware that he had perhaps reached the point at which his thoughts became slightly less reliable than usual. He knew that he was inclined to be overly suspicious, but that inclination had kept him alive this long. And where James was concerned, he saw no reason not to let every spark of worry kindle itself into a full-blown conflagration.

Cora's rheumy blue eyes drifted away from Edith and settled on Leo. "You look ghastly," she told him, not unkindly.

"I feel ghastly," he agreed. "Tell me more about this Rupert Bellamy." He knew that Cora and Edith would know he was asking, more or less, for a dossier. It was easy to forget that Cora, for all she was now a pink-cheeked old lady, once had a job not so different from Leo's. She had retired and now spent her days by a warm fire with the person she loved. Leo didn't know how she had done it. That sort of transformation seemed about as probable as a bat transforming into a pigeon.

"He married Charlotte Sommers, James's father's sister," said Cora.

"She had twelve bridesmaids at her wedding. Quite a foolish woman," said Edith. "Sickly, I believe. Died ages ago. As for Rupert, Cora's quite right. A very boring man."

"The only interesting thing that happened to him wasn't even his doing," Cora said. "What was his daughter's name?" she asked, turning to Edith. "Not Lady Marchand, but the one who disappeared. Rosalind? Rosalie?"

"Rose. Must be twenty years now. 1927 or so. And she didn't disappear, Cora. She had a swimming accident."

"Is that right? I always hoped she ran off with the chauffeur," Cora sighed.

"Yes, well the papers could hardly have run the story for two straight weeks without some romantic angle. But it turned out that the chauffeur—you know, Cora, I think he might have been a gardener or a groom, not a chauffeur."

"It was always one of those three, when a girl ran away with a servant," Cora observed. "I do wonder who girls run away with these days."

The women paused, as if observing a moment of silence for modern girls who had to make do in unknown ways.

"In any event," Edith said, "I believe they said the chauffeur or gardener or groom ran off because he got a girl in trouble and it had nothing at all to do with Rose. Sadly prosaic."

"What a good memory you have, dear. All I can really recall is Reverend Sommers having to leave in the middle of the village fete in order to fetch James. The curate had to step in and man the coconut shy."

"And what a sorry affair *that* was," Edith agreed.

What had been a slight sense of unease now developed into alarm. "Fetch James from where?" Leo asked. "James was there when this girl died? And he's been summoned back?" Now Leo was worried about something far more probable than poisoned tea. Sometimes even the thought of violent death stirred up memories of war that James couldn't quite shake off. James was a grown man and could handle his own mind's idiosyncrasies, but if Leo could do anything to help, then he'd make it his business to do so.

CHAPTER THREE

As he made his way toward the drawing room, James encountered detail after familiar detail. The carpet at the top of the stairs; the painting of a rather mangy-looking dog hanging opposite his bedroom door; the wallpaper with a pattern that looked peculiarly like faces. He hadn't thought about any of these things for years, but evidently Blackthorn existed in a corner of his mind, intact and undisturbed, sealed tight with a layer of dust, even though he hadn't thought about it in decades.

He supposed it could have felt like a homecoming of sorts, but instead, each remembered detail made James feel vaguely queasy—which, in turn, made him feel oddly guilty and ungrateful, as if he were still the orphaned child here on sufferance.

Even before pushing open the heavy door, James heard the crisp tones of a cut-glass accent emanating from inside the drawing room.

"Not a fire lit in the whole house," the woman said, her voice a drawl that split the difference between amusement and irritation. "And I forgot, if you can credit it, Lilah darling, that your grandfather never put in central heating. We always come in summer, of course, and one doesn't think to ask. Why on earth Martha didn't put her foot down, I cannot imagine. We all know what Father was, but you'd think that with him gone she'd at the very least light a fire."

James hesitated on the threshold, his hand poised to open the door, but not quite ready to enter. That voice. It was his cousin Camilla, of course: Lady Marchand, Uncle Rupert's only surviving daughter. It could hardly be anybody else. They had run into one another in London a few times before the war—once at the theater, once when James was taking a girl out to dinner, back when he still was trying to convince himself that he wanted to do that sort of thing. What James remembered most from these meetings was Camilla's rich attire and the general air of money that seemed to follow her around like a cloud. She always seemed vaguely surprised to discover that James still existed, despite having spent every summer with him until he was twelve and then sending him a handful of birthday cards when he was still at school, sometimes with a crisp five-pound note folded inside.

James opened the door in time to hear a much quieter female voice respond.

"I daresay Aunt Martha is used to being uncomfortable, Mother," said a slim, platinum-haired woman who sat straight-backed on the sofa. "She's spent thirty years at Blackthorn, which is long enough to accustom one to all manner of inconvenience."

"You only say that because you don't remember what Black-thorn used to be. Poor Martha," sighed Camilla. James hadn't remembered her as being particularly striking as a young woman—compared to Rose, everyone else seemed faded and unremarkable. But whatever had been the case twenty years ago, in her early forties, Camilla was very handsome. Her dark hair was fashionably dressed beneath a smart black hat. She wore a tailored gray dress and matching cardigan that suggested, rather than announced, mourning. The girl on the sofa must then be her daughter, Lilian. He had never met her, as she had not yet arrived on the scene that final summer he spent at Blackthorn. That meant she must now be at most twenty.

James deployed his warmest smile, the one he used for stubborn patients and ornery nurses. "Hullo," he said, awkwardly hovering in the doorway and rather wishing Martha were there to smooth over the introductions. How was one meant to introduce oneself to one's own relations? "I don't suppose you remember me." He regretted the words immediately—it was as if being at Blackthorn had transformed him back into into the shy and diffident child he had once been, a boy used to being shuffled among aunts and uncles during school holidays, forever on his best manners.

But Camilla turned to face James, turning on him a pair of bright blue eyes only slightly obscured by gold-rimmed spectacles. "Of course I remember you, James. Don't be absurd. You're the very image of your father."

James sucked in a breath. He was used to people sidestepping the issue of his father.

"Camilla," murmured a man in a tone of unmistakable reproach.

James turned to see Sir Anthony Marchand rise to his feet. He was at least ten years older than his wife, with thick gray hair and piercing blue eyes. Sir Anthony had risen to prominence as a Harley Street psychiatrist, although James still remembered when he had been referred to in hushed tones as a nerve specialist. Before marrying Camilla, he had attended James's own father in the private asylum where Theodore Sommers had been sent after the war. As a child, James had never warmed to him, possibly because of associations with his father's absence, or simply because Marchand had only rarely joined in sailing and swimming and playing tennis.

But as an adult, and as a physician himself, he knew that Sir Anthony Marchand was considered the best, and when James, in a fit of desperation after his own war, needed help, he had sought out Marchand.

James preferred not to think about that appointment.

"One can hardly escape noticing the likeness," said Camilla, whose gaze hadn't left James since he entered the room.

"No need to mention such things," Sir Anthony said to his wife, his voice pitched low enough that James might almost believe he wasn't meant to hear, but then the older man glanced apologetically at James.

Camilla removed her glasses and slid them into her handbag, and James repressed a sigh. Sir Anthony, like so many people, believed that it was better to pretend that James's father had never existed. Perhaps he believed that suicide shouldn't be alluded to in a civilized drawing room, or perhaps he believed that James would go to pieces at the slightest provocation. Or maybe he just didn't like being reminded of a patient he had lost.

He hadn't had any such scruples two years earlier, when James visited him at his plush Harley Street office. Then Sir Anthony had employed phrases like *unfortunate family history of mental imbalance* and *best to err on the side of caution* and *it's quite a nice sort of place, more like a spa than a hospital.*

James mustered up all his cordiality and shook hands with

the older man. "Good to see you, Sir Anthony."

"You look well," the older man responded, grasping James's hand firmly.

"Mother," said the girl on the sofa. "Do keep your spectacles on. You're missing the ashtray by a yard."

Only then did James turn his attention away from Sir Anthony to the young woman. She had fine features and white-blond hair so fair as to be nearly silver and wore a dark blue tailor-made. He had the distinct impression that he had met her before. "You must be my cousin Lilian."

She seemed to notice James's confusion and laughed, a broad smile transforming her face from an almost pre-Raphaelite languor to a vivaciousness that made James smile automatically in return. "You probably know me as Lilah Fairchild. Do call me Lilah. Everybody does."

It took James a moment to make sense of her words and understand that he was shaking the hand of an actress he had seen on stage and screen. "I saw you last month in *Twelfth Night*," James said, feeling faintly starstruck. He and Leo had taken the train into London for a matinee. "It was splendid, not that you need me to tell you so. I had no idea you were Camilla's daughter." Obviously, he had not recognized her stage name, nor had he detected any family likeness, since Lilah's fairylike beauty was so unlike the robust, dark handsomeness of the Bellamys. He'd have thought she got her looks from her father's side, but one glance at the strong features and solid frame of Sir Anthony was enough to dispel that notion.

"We keep the family connection quiet," Lilah said, her gaze darting to where her father stood nearby.

Before James could figure out what that meant, Sir Anthony

interrupted.

"You still have that little practice of yours?" he asked James.

"Yes," James said, forcing politeness. The man spoke as if James's medical practice was an embarrassing hobby. Being a village doctor might not have been what James once thought he'd do with his life, but it was satisfying and it was a chance to do some good in the world. He said none of this. "I do."

"Hmm," Sir Anthony said, as if examining a troubling rash.

The door swung open again and Martha entered, visibly flustered and carrying a tray of tea things. "I'm so sorry to keep you waiting."

"Stop talking like you're a housemaid, Martha," Camilla said, lighting another cigarette and making no effort to take the tray from Martha's arms. "You're not here to serve us."

Martha made a sound that sounded to James's ears like disbelief. "Well, here's tea, such as it is. Oh, thank you, Jamie, just put it on the coffee table."

"I'll warn you, James," Camilla said. "It'll be stale scones and a packet of digestive biscuits. Mrs. Carrow is a very good cook, but her arrangement is that she only does dinner. These days one can't really set one's own terms with the help, can one?"

"I suppose not," James said. He had been more or less fending for himself since his cleaner was murdered the previous autumn, but that had more to do with his reluctance to have anyone poking around his house and discovering that Leo didn't sleep in the spare room than it did any difficulty in finding suitable help.

"One takes what one can get. Martha, darling, what are you going to do now?" Camilla asked. "You can't mean to stay on at Blackthorn all alone, can you?"

James watched irritation flash across Martha's face. This was the familiar and justifiable impatience of the poor when confronted with rich people who can't bring themselves to understand how everybody else lives. Between the small fortune she'd inherited from her mother and the handsome income her husband no doubt brought in, Camilla Marchand had probably never needed to trouble herself with such questions as whether she would have a roof over her head in a week's time.

James thought there was something else in Martha's irritation, something that went beyond pounds and shillings, but he couldn't quite identify it.

Whatever annoyance Martha felt with her cousin, she swept it away and adopted a neutral tone—indeed, one very much like he'd expect from a housekeeper whose wages depended on her pleasant manner. "Whether I can stay on at Blackthorn depends on who the house goes to."

"I—oh, I see." Camilla absently tapped her cigarette on the edge of the ashtray, causing ash to scatter all over the tabletop and drift to the carpet. "I had thought—well, never mind what I had thought."

James assumed that Blackthorn would go to Camilla, as Uncle Rupert's sole surviving child. And probably Camilla had been under the same impression. Now she had a line between her eyebrows, and an awkward silence fell over the drawing room.

What they all needed was tea, and since nobody had started to pour it out, James decided to take matters into his own hands, distributing cups of dismayingly weak tea.

Lilah drummed her vermilion fingernails on the arm of the sofa. "I suppose that if Granddad meant to keep things simple, he wouldn't have made a point of this circus."

"Lillian," her father said warningly.

"Well, it's true," Lilah said, ignoring her father's tone. She reached for her mother's cigarette case, helping herself before offering it to James. "If he meant to be reasonable about it, he would at least have told Mother about his plans ages ago. It's not as if he died suddenly. Poor Granddad was extremely ancient." She let James light her cigarette. "I dare say none of it's going to be what we expect."

As if on cue, a knock sounded at the front door and Martha sprang to her feet. She returned a moment later with a woman so dissimilar from the ladies already gathered in the drawing room as to seem like a specimen from an unrelated species. She wore what appeared to be an old-fashioned tea gown of purple velvet and a great quantity of scarves. Her hair was hennaed to a bright red and she wore no hat. She could have been any age between thirty-five and fifty-five.

"This is Madame Fournier," Martha said, the name awkward on her tongue in a way that suggested the new arrival was a stranger in the house.

"A pleasure," said Madame Fournier in thickly accented English.

For an awkward moment, everyone stared at Madame Fournier as if absorbing how out of place she was among the Sevres and Aubussons of the Blackthorn drawing room. Everyone seemed to expect somebody else to take charge. Camilla plainly expected Martha to act as hostess, while Martha expected Camilla to do the same. As for Sir Anthony, he probably thought awkward silences were psychologically edifying.

James flung himself into the breach. "Have some tea,

22

Madame," he said. "Sugar?"

When James glanced up as he handed Madame her tea, he saw an elderly man standing in the open doorway, carrying a sheaf of papers. He had sparse white hair and a weathered face partly obscured by a pair of thick spectacles. Even at a distance of several yards, James could see that the papers shook in the man's grip. This had to be the solicitor, Mr. Trevelyan. He was very old, at least eighty; twenty years ago, he would still have seemed very old to a twelve-year-old James.

Martha went to him and relieved him of his papers, then led him to a wingback chair near the fireplace—which, James couldn't help but think, would have been a kinder gesture if the fireplace had contained an actual fire or even an electric one.

"It's nearly five," James heard Martha tell the solicitor, "so the Carrows will come up shortly and then we can start. They're the couple who live in the lodge and look after Blackthorn," she added, seemingly for James's benefit.

"They were mentioned in Rupert's will, so they ought to be present," Mr. Trevelyan added.

No sooner had the words been spoken then two more people entered the room, a man and a woman.

"I beg your pardon, Miss Dauntsey," said the woman, addressing Martha. "Had to get the roast in the oven." In one hand she clutched what appeared to be a hastily removed apron. She had a soft West Indian accent, and was about thirty, Black, and plump. She was pleasant looking, with an air of competence about her that made James feel optimistic about dinner. The man by her side was a little bit older, with skin that might originally have been fair but was darkened by what looked like a lifetime spent in the sun. He was dressed for the outdoors, including a cap that he didn't remove. Instead of sitting, they stood by the door—not, James thought, out of deference, but from a reluctance to be any more involved in the proceedings than strictly necessary.

James's attention was on the Carrows, so he couldn't have said exactly what happened or who was responsible, but Madame Fournier's teacup, which a moment before had been safe in her hand, was now shattered on the floor, its contents distributed between the carpet and Sir Anthony's trouser leg.

"Oh dear," Martha said, looking around futilely for something to mop up the spill. Sir Anthony dabbed ineffectively at his trouser leg with a pocket handkerchief. James managed to extract the tea towel from the tray without upending the teapot, and handed it to Sir Anthony, who took it without thanks.

A clock then began to chime, loud enough to bring any conversation to a standstill. It was the tall casement clock in the hall, James recalled, able to picture it vividly. It tolled five times, during which the assembled guests mostly avoided looking at one another.

"I won't take up too much of your time," Mr. Trevelyan said. His voice was thin and shaky, but it carried across the drawing room. "The late Rupert Bellamy's will was quite simple." He took a pair of spectacles from his pocket and balanced them on his nose. "To my wife's cousin Martha Dauntsey, in recognition of her devotion, I leave two hundred pounds and an annuity of fifty pounds a year."

James tried not to look as if he were watching Martha for a reaction, but he didn't see her face register any reaction. Fifty pounds a year was no mean thing, but it was not enough to live on unless Martha were to abide in shabbier circumstances than he could imagine any relation of his—or of any of the Bellamys—willingly inhabiting.

The solicitor continued. "To my daughter, Camilla Marchand, I leave the Gainsborough that hangs in the dining room at Blackthorn."

Camilla looked like she was about to speak, presumably to ask what was to become of the rest of Blackthorn's contents as well as the house itself, but Mr. Trevelyan didn't pause.

"To my wife's nephew, James Sommers, I leave the photograph of his father on Coronation Day in 1911."

James hadn't known such a thing existed. Bequeathing James a photograph of a man who had been so thoroughly erased from the family history seemed at best a mixed blessing. A sick feeling began to gather in the pit of his stomach.

"To Reverend—" Mr. Trevelyan broke off. "We can pass over that bequest, as the legatee is not present."

He cleared his throat and continued. "To Miriam and Henry Carrow, I leave one hundred pounds in recognition of their service. To anyone who was employed at Blackthorn in 1927, I leave one hundred pounds, if they can provide proof of their identity and employment so as to satisfy the law firm of Trevelyan and Hodges, Plymouth."

At the mention of 1927, the room, which had already been quiet, went utterly still.

Mr. Trevelyan looked up and peered at his audience over the rims of his spectacles. "That part of the will is straightforward. The next part is also straightforward, but unconventional." He returned his attention to the paper before him. "The residue of my estate, including the property of Blackthorn as detailed in Appendix A and the contents of the bank accounts and financial assets detailed in Appendix B, I leave to whichever of those named above and present the day this document is read discovers what happened to Rose Bellamy on the first of August, 1927."

For the space of two heartbeats the room was utterly silent. James saw Martha's hands gripping the arms of her chair so hard that her knuckles were white. He saw Camilla's mouth hang open. Sir Anthony's face darkened to an alarming shade of puce. Even Lilah's face was grave. From where James sat, he could not see Madame Fournier or the Carrows without turning his head, which he managed to resist doing.

"There's one final clause. In the event that no satisfactory solution has been presented to Robert Trevelyan or his representatives at the stroke of noon, two days after the reading of this will, the residue of the estate, including Blackthorn and all its contents, is to be held in trust for the Society for the Reformation of Young Delinquents."

Another silence fell, during which James heard nothing but the ticking of the grandfather clock.

CHAPTER FOUR

I t was the work of ten minutes for Leo to let himself into James's house, shower off the grime of travel, change into something from James's side of the wardrobe (he couldn't help it if James's clothes were just *nicer*), help himself to James's car keys, and take off in a general southwesterly direction. Only then did he bother to devise a pretense for visiting this godforsaken Cornish country house that James had taken himself off to.

The sun was low in the sky when Leo finally rolled into the drive, the house backlit in a way that rendered it a mere silhouette and stripped it of any detail. It looked frankly ominous, but Leo supposed all houses looked ominous under these conditions.

It was an awkward hour, just the time when most households were sitting down to dinner or clearing up afterward, and nobody came to the door when Leo knocked. There was no light at the front door except what came from the setting sun, but Leo's pocket torch revealed no sign of any kind of doorbell. He knocked yet again, this time hard enough to make his ungloved knuckles smart. But his persistence was rewarded and the door swung open, revealing James himself.

For an instant, Leo knew that everything he felt was written across his face—relief at seeing James safe and sound, relief at seeing James at all, and the dawning comprehension that he had behaved like an utter maniac by driving across the country to arrive uninvited at the home of a stranger. If this had been a job, he would have blown his cover in that unguarded half second.

He watched James for any sign that he was less than delighted by Leo's arrival. Instead, though, a flicker of something bright and candid crossed James's face before he checked himself. Leo had the distinct sense that if it hadn't been for the chance of being observed, James might have taken him in his arms. Leo's heart gave a wild, happy leap in his chest, something he had not known it was capable of until he met James. The sweetness of James's reaction made Leo feel vaguely fraudulent, as if he had succeeded in passing off a bad penny to an innocent shopkeeper.

"I learned you were in the neighborhood and decided to call on you," Leo murmured. "All the other details are the same."

James gave a quick nod. "Mr. Page," he said, loudly enough to carry and in a creditable simulation of politely repressed surprise, "what *can* you be doing at Blackthorn?"

"I'm visiting my sister in Looe," Leo said, matching his tone. He had no sister, either in Looe or anywhere else, and James knew it. "And Miss Pickering rang to tell us that you were only minutes away. Of course Susan insisted that I motor over to give you her love and to ask you for tea tomorrow."

"I should love nothing more than to see Susan," James said. "We've just finished dinner. Do come in for some coffee."

Leo followed James across the stone floor of an imposing hall to a sitting room filled with people who, to Leo's relief, did not seem to be actively engaged in attempts to slip poisons into one another's drinks. In short order, Leo found himself being introduced to this odd assemblage of guests, James simply presenting him as Mr. Page, a friend from home.

Leo assessed each person he met. A grim-faced but rather distractingly attractive doctor. His wife, a dark-haired woman with the most appallingly posh accent. Their daughter, who was none other than the actress who played Viola in the production of *Twelfth Night* that he and James had seen the previous month. A mousy, middle-aged spinster who Leo gathered was a sort of fixture in the house, and who looked as tired as Leo felt. A—good God—what was that creature with all the scarves? And a man so old and frail he looked to be at death's door.

At first glance it seemed to be an ordinary family group with two glaringly obvious outsiders—the actress and the woman who looked like somebody's idea of a fortune teller. But evidently the actress was in fact family. And James, who appeared to be family, only barely was. The entire picture was slightly off, just enough to set Leo's teeth on edge.

"You look well," James said when the introductions were complete. A stranger might not have noticed the question lurking in that statement.

"I'm quite well," Leo said. And he was. No serious injuries, no imminent likelihood of foreign governments trying to assassinate him in his sleep—he was as well as he'd ever been.

"You might be interested to hear about the peculiar situation in which we all find ourselves," James said casually. As James recounted the contents of his uncle's will and the challenge the legatees had been issued, the uneasiness that had been lurking in Leo's gut solidified into real fear.

"How very thrilling," he said instead of dragging James out of the house and taking him someplace safe.

"It can't be legally binding," interjected the doctor, a Sir Anthony somebody-or-another, in a tone that made Leo think he had been repeating the same phrase intermittently for hours. "We'll challenge it in court," Sir Anthony went on. "He must have become senile. It happens, however little we like to admit it. Rather negligent on your firm's part, Trevelyan, to let him follow through with this delusional scheme of his."

"He wasn't in the least bit senile," said the spinster, whom James had introduced as Miss Dauntsey but addressed as Cousin Martha.

"Even if that were true, how is anyone to verify what happened twenty years ago?" the doctor continued. "There won't be any proof. This estate will spend an eternity in probate."

"An excellent question," said the ancient lawyer with the air of a teacher congratulating an apt pupil. "Mr. Bellamy's will included a proviso that I am to be the judge of the solution."

"In other words," said Lady Marchand, the doctor's wife, "he's leaving it up to you to decide who gets it all."

Mr. Trevelyan cleared his throat. "I rather think your father would say that he was leaving it up to you."

And wasn't that an interesting way to put it. Clearly James's uncle had thought one of his legatees knew what had happened to his daughter all those years ago, and it sounded like the solicitor was of the same mind.

Cora and Edith—whom Leo was usually inclined to trust on all matters of intelligence—said that Rose Bellamy was popularly understood to have died in a swimming accident. Had her father suspected that someone had been to blame for the accident? Or had he believed that there was a more sinister explanation for his daughter's death?

"The way I see it," said Lady Marchand, "is that we'd better abide by Father's little scheme. Otherwise somebody else might go to Mr. Trevelyan with any manner of likely-sounding solution, and then Blackthorn could go to a stranger." She glanced vaguely at Madame Fournier, not with any particular enmity, but more as if she had forgotten that the woman could hear her. "Or to that charity. Imagine Blackthorn packed to the rafters with lady criminals."

"It's a very respectable charity, Camilla. I've spent my career—"

"I'm rather enjoying the image of Blackthorn packed with lady criminals," said the actress, with a faraway look that made Leo want to laugh.

"There is no need for you to flaunt the—the *deviance* of the company you keep, Lilian," snapped her father.

"This is all too bad for you, Martha darling," said Camilla, ignoring both her daughter and her husband. "You've been done out of a house. You'll come stay with us in London, of course."

"It's proof that poor Rupert was not in his right mind," Sir Anthony said severely, glaring at Mr. Trevelyan. "I do wish someone had thought to call me in. I deal with senility cases with some frequency, after all."

Leo watched as James hesitated with his coffee cup halfway to his mouth. A fleeting, pinched expression darted across his features.

"I assure you that Mr. Bellamy's own doctor attended him almost daily," said Mr. Trevelyan.

"I intend to give that doctor a piece of my mind if he failed to notice an imbalance."

"I did always covet that Gainsborough," mused Lady Marchand. "It's rather sweet that the old dear remembered, even if he was out of his head at the end."

"That's hardly the point, Camilla," her husband barked. "I dare say the bequests aren't inane if taken individually. Martha is probably glad to have been left more than an ordinary servant, for example."

Lilah and James both snapped their attention to Sir Anthony. A glint of ice-cold fury was in the girl's eyes while James only looked shocked. Martha Dauntsey, meanwhile, hardly seemed to register the slight.

"Mr. Trevelyan," said Lilah, "when did my grandfather make this will?"

"It's dated June of last year," said the solicitor. "Although he didn't send it to the office. Miss Dauntsey found it among his papers. But it was properly signed and witnessed."

"I see," said Lilah with a thoughtful look.

"Besides, we already know what happened to Rose," said Sir Anthony, as if neither the solicitor nor his daughter had spoken. "It was all decided quite certainly that summer. The police were involved. She died in a swimming accident."

Leo wanted to curse the naivete of anyone who had reached Marchand's age without learning exactly how easily the police could be bamboozled by the simple expedients of coordinated lying, a bit of fast talking, and cold hard cash.

"In fact," Marchand continued, "I'm prepared to offer Mr. Trevelyan a solution right now. Rose died by misadventure, precisely as the police said. Her mind was sadly unbalanced, and as a result, she went for a swim at a time when she ought to have known the tide would be too strong, however good a swimmer she might have been. All very unfortunate."

This was the second time Marchand had used the word *imbalance,* and Leo's thoughts caught on it. The late Mr. Bellamy had been imbalanced; the dead girl was imbalanced. But in this context the meaning was clear—nobody spoke of someone's death by supposed misadventure and simultaneously alluded to their imbalanced mental state unless they meant the person had taken their own life. Before Leo could wonder what evidence might have been presented to the police—a body, a note, a witness—he heard James set his coffee cup back into its saucer with rather more of a clatter than usual. That was all the sign Leo needed. He rose to his feet.

"Well, I'd better be off before Susan worries," Leo said, addressing James. "Won't you walk me out?"

As soon as they were outside and at a comfortable distance from the house, Leo spoke. "Get out of there. Come with me. Say you long to see Susan. We'll have you engaged to my imaginary sister before the night is out."

James laughed and bumped his shoulder against Leo's. "I can't. If my uncle's last wish was for this to happen, then I can spare a couple of days."

"Last wish, my arse. He's not around anymore to get a say in what you do. And that lot in there are a disaster waiting to happen."

"That's why I need to stay, though. They need a civilizing presence. Wait." They had reached the parked car.

"Well, that's your car," Leo said awkwardly. "I think I might have stolen it, by the way."

"No, I don't mean the car. The tree."

Leo followed James's gaze to a bare-branched tree, likely a fruit tree of some kind.

"That didn't used to be there," James said. "I've spent half the day cataloguing things that are exactly as they were twenty years ago, and now there's an entire new tree. Who puts a cherry tree next to the garage? And on the north side, too. It can't get nearly enough sun."

"Wendy is rubbing off on you with all this gardening wisdom."

James bumped Leo with his elbow, then seemed to realize that they were standing next to his car.

"Leo. Did you drive my car all the way from Wychcomb St. Mary?"

"Afraid so." Leo adopted a studiedly casual tone. "Otherwise I would have had to either change trains in Reading or get a taxi to Cheltenham. This was much faster."

James looked at him, and Leo knew that he was reading between the lines well enough to hear all the want and concern that had fueled Leo's hurried drive to Cornwall.

"I hope you don't mind," Leo said. "I know I'm intruding. And I took your car without permission."

"I don't mind. You're welcome to anything of mine. You know that."

James had said as much before, although not in so many words. Leo had long since decided not to take that sentiment at face value. James was determined to fling open the door to his cozy life as if Leo could simply walk in and make himself at home. And Leo didn't know how to explain to James that this wasn't possible without thoroughly disillusioning the man. "If you won't come with me, then let me stay here with you."

James raised his eyebrows. "What excuse would we give to them?" He gestured toward the house.

Leo reached into his pocket and retrieved a blackened metal

object. "My carburetor cap. I took the precaution of removing it before turning into the drive. When I leave, I'll have engine trouble before I reach the road. If you don't want me to stay, it'll be a simple matter of screwing the cap back on before I get in the car. Otherwise, I'll be back in a quarter of an hour, and your cousin will no doubt offer me a room for the night"

"You'll probably have to bunk with me. Cousin Martha is already short on room."

"You say that as if it'll put me off," Leo said, shaking his head. "I haven't seen you in two weeks."

"Your trip." James spoke carefully, as he always did when alluding to Leo's work. "Was it very bad?"

Leo quickly shook his head. "It was fine." A gust of wind blew across the drive, making them both draw their coats across their chests and carrying with it a faint hint of salt, the only reminder of how close they were to the sea.

"I'm glad you're back," James said. "I'm glad you're here."

Well, that was probably just because he hadn't yet realized how abnormally Leo was behaving. Leo felt that he ought to point that out, but instead flicked the brim of his hat and winked. "See you in a couple of minutes."

CHAPTER FIVE

Over half an hour passed, and still Leo hadn't returned. James's first thought, naturally, was that the car had exploded. He had no idea what carburetor caps did and doubted that their sole function was to prevent explosions, but that did little to put his mind at ease. Historically, his mind was not much inclined toward anything resembling ease in the first place, and during the past two months he had learned to live with a constant thrum of worry where Leo was concerned.

Earlier, he had watched Leo move, looking for signs of injury, and thought he saw some stiffness on the man's left side. There were certainly faint circles under Leo's eyes and a palpable weariness about him. He looked like he needed a couple of aspirins and some comfortable pajamas, and then to be tucked in to bed and left there for a long while.

The last time Leo returned from a mission, James had been at his kitchen table, about to have a solitary dinner of tinned soup and toast. When he answered the door and saw Leo, he had abandoned the soup and taken Leo straight to bed. He was extremely annoyed that he couldn't do that now. He ought to have taken Leo up on the offer to leave Blackthorn. They would be home by midnight, and Leo could sleep as late as he pleased in James's bed.

Another quarter of an hour passed, during which time a bottle of whiskey materialized courtesy of Sir Anthony. If nothing else, the man at least had the good sense to produce hard drink when the occasion called for it. James concluded that if there had been an explosion, he probably would have heard it, which offered some comfort.

A knock sounded at the door, but it was only Mr. Trevelyan's driver arriving to take him home. James couldn't sit still, so he paced the room, smoked a cigarette, pretended to look out the window, and then had another cigarette.

In any other circumstance, James's edgy mood might be glaringly obvious, but nearly everyone else in the drawing room seemed either preoccupied or as nervous as James was. Lilah and Cousin Martha sat together on the sofa, discussing Lilah's upcoming film. In a wingback chair, Sir Anthony leafed through a newspaper, turning the pages almost violently. Camilla lounged on an old-fashioned settee with her eyes half shut.

Madame Fournier approached James at the window. "When the night is so dark," she said, her accent generically Continental and impossible to pin down, "a window is nothing more than a mirror. You do not strike me as a vain man, Dr. Sommers. Perhaps there is something else you regard in the window?"

Good Lord. What was a man meant to say to something like that? "Just debating whether it'll be too cold to walk to the sea in the morning," he said, aiming for bluff good cheer.

"It seems to me," she answered, "that you and I are the only ones who find these goings on—how does one say—amiss? The little fair-haired one, she thinks it is droll. The rich ones, they think it is an annoyance. But you and I, we know it is wrong."

This seemed quite impertinent, and even more so for being accurate. For twenty years, James had believed that Rose died in a swimming accident, and for almost as long he had understood this swimming accident to be a polite fiction disguising a suicide. He tried to remember why he was so certain of this, and had to wonder if it was simply because her death was hushed up in the same way his father's had been, and took place only a few months later.

But if Uncle Rupert believed that something else had happened to Rose, James was entirely at sea.

"Who would have wanted to do away with Miss Bellamy?" asked Madame Fournier, giving voice to the suspicion that James hadn't wanted to think about.

He dug his fingernails into the meat of his palm and drained the rest of his whiskey. "I beg your pardon," he said, aware that he was resorting to stuffiness because he had no other sane manner of reacting.

Instead of looking at the strange woman beside him, he fixed his gaze on a vase of dried chrysanthemums that sat on the chimneypiece. The mums looked dusty and might have been picked any autumn in the past twenty years. The vase—a dark green art nouveau number with painted lilies—James remembered distinctly, as it had always been in precisely that place.

And then he realized why all these remembered details had unsettled him: under ordinary circumstances, houses didn't remain unchanged for twenty years. Paintings were moved around. Carpets became too worn to be serviceable and were replaced or removed. Walls were repapered. Vases were shifted from the mantle to the sideboard.

Blackthorn hadn't been preserved; it had been left to molder.

He had always assumed that life at Blackthorn carried on much as usual even after he was sent away, even after Rose was gone. He had supposed that the whirl of picnics and tennis and parties and dancing continued. But it seemed that Blackthorn had stopped living in 1927.

"It is what everyone is thinking," said Madame, dragging James back to 1948. She was either unaware of or unbothered by James's rebuff. "Or, it ought to be. It is certainly what I am thinking."

James's gaze traveled to Martha, who sat on the couch, pulling at a loose loop of yarn in her cardigan as Lilah gesticulated animatedly. "You're wrong," he said abruptly. "I mean, you and I aren't the only ones worried. Martha—Miss Dauntsey—is worried too."

"Worried?" Madame eyed him curiously. "That is not what I said. But yes, you are worried, I see that. Miss Dauntsey, she is not worried. She is distressed, and it is not new. It has nothing to do with the will or this gathering."

James raised his eyebrows. "I was under the impression that you hadn't met one another before today."

"One can see that she wears her worry like an old coat."

"Do I wear my worry like an old coat?" James asked, mostly to himself. He desperately wished that Leo would hurry up, because he had a most alarming suspicion that this conversation was about to take a turn toward the spirits of the vasty deep and he was too tipsy to keep a straight face. "How did you say you knew my uncle?" he asked. The more this woman talked, the less he could imagine her having anything to do with any Bellamy, alive or dead. She had to be one of the former Blackthorn servants mentioned in Uncle Rupert's will, but James didn't see how that could be possible without Camilla or Martha recognizing her.

"I didn't," she said, and before he could press her, James heard the front door open and shut, followed by the sounds of conversation drifting in from the hall.

James could recognize Leo's voice—a trifle louder and heartier than usual, decidedly alive and not the victim of an explosion—but also that of another man.

Carrow appeared in the drawing room door looking apologetic and still wearing his heavy coat and flat cap. "Mr. Page's car broke down," he said to Martha. With that, he made a perfunctory gesture toward the brim of his cap, clapped Leo on the shoulder, and took his leave. Well, that was Leo. James supposed Leo had been given a hot supper and also the Carrows' life story in the past hour or so.

"I do beg your pardon," Leo said to Martha. "But can I use your telephone to ring up a taxi? I suppose the village has lodgings of some sort. Failing that, I'll get the taxi to bring me back to Looe."

Martha looked up, her brow creased with worry. "Goodness. Do stay here for the night. We ought to have an empty room, because not everyone came who Mr. Trevelyan expected."

"I'm afraid not," said Lilah. "I wasn't invited—I'm afraid I crashed the party and took over the empty room."

"There's the blue room, then. It has that leak in the ceiling but it isn't raining, and the window only rattles a little."

"We won't put Mr. Page in the dreadful blue room," Lilah said. "I can bunk in with Mother. After all, it's my arrival that's made you short on habitable rooms."

Well, that would never do. "Mr. Page can sleep on the sofa

in my room," James said, hoping he didn't sound too eager.

"That's settled, then," said Martha, looking relieved.

When Leo approached James at the window, it was with a glass in one hand and the bottle of whiskey in the other.

James held out his glass for Leo to fill and their gaze caught. James wanted to admit that he had been stupid with worry, for the past hour and the past fortnight. He wanted to admit that he didn't know these people anymore, if he ever had, and that he didn't want to be with them. But instead he prepared himself to follow through with the rest of their charade in case anyone was listening. "I hope your car isn't too badly damaged."

"I haven't a clue," said Leo. "Great clouds of black smoke billowed up from the bonnet. Most alarming. The gardener chap said the carburetor is in a devilish poor state but that he'll give it a look tomorrow."

James took a drink of his whiskey. "Do you need to ring up Susan and let her know what happened?" He always felt like such a fumbling idiot when attempting to meet Leo lie for lie. He was terrible at it, the tips of his ears heating with every falsehood.

"I already phoned her from the lodge," Leo said easily.

The clock chimed ten and Sir Anthony got to his feet. He was the sort of man who couldn't get out of a chair or walk across a room without making his presence known. He wasn't loud or lumbering; it was just, as much as James hated to acknowledge it, a sort of innate charisma. Good looks too, he noted in irritation. This was probably why the great and good of the land sought him out whenever a member of the family began hearing voices or acting in an alarming way. He just had a presence. Not a soothing presence, and certainly nothing that

41

could be referred to as a pleasant bedside manner. It was more that he seemed like he could frighten off whatever troubles afflicted his patients. Hundreds of years ago, he would have been precisely the sort of priest one would want to perform an exorcism.

"It's been a long day and I'm for bed," Sir Anthony announced, with enough force that James nearly headed to the doorway himself. With a perfunctory "good night" aimed at everyone and no one, Sir Anthony left the room, Camilla and Lilah trailing behind him. Martha and Madame Fournier followed a moment later. And finally, finally, James was alone with Leo.

CHAPTER SIX

"**S**hall we head upstairs as well?" James asked, coming to sit beside Leo on the sofa—not so close that they'd need to spring apart if anyone walked in, but close enough that they hardly needed to speak above a whisper to hear one another. Close enough, too, that he could give Leo's arm a quick squeeze, which is exactly what he did. "You look knackered."

"I am, and then some." Leo stretched an arm along the back of the sofa, his fingers briefly resting on the nape of James's neck. "But no, I don't want to go to bed yet. The lawyer left his papers on the writing desk and I mean to read them as soon as I can be sure nobody will interrupt me."

"Fine by me," James said, refilling both their glasses and letting his fingers brush along Leo's wrist as he did so.

Leo closed his eyes and tipped his head against the back of the sofa.

"When was the last time you slept?" James asked.

"I might have dozed on the airplane," Leo said.

"In a bed, Leo."

"Wednesday, I think." Leo didn't open his eyes.

That actually wasn't as bad as James had feared. "It's

rather lovely to have you here," James said, conscious that this was a drastic understatement. It was shocking enough that he got to have Leo at home; the idea that Leo might turn up elsewhere seemed almost too good to be true. In December they had—stumblingly, mortifyingly—agreed that they enjoyed being together in and out of bed and agreed to keep doing that. But surely it couldn't be that simple. Surely James didn't get to have someone like Leo in his life and keep him there just because he wanted it. "I was dreading this weekend."

One of the corners of Leo's mouth ticked up in a tired smile. "A reading of the will. For God's sake, James. I half expected to find you all shooting one another. Cabinets of exotic poisons left unlocked. Sharpened daggers mounted above the chimneypiece."

"Ah. I see. You came for the entertainment potential."

Leo breathed out a laugh and rolled his head to face James. His tired eyes were still mostly closed and he regarded James through dark eyelashes. "You know why I came."

James felt his cheeks heat and wondered if he'd ever get used to Leo saying these things. It happened so rarely and never with any warning. A man simply couldn't build up any kind of natural immunity.

"Do you want to get to the bottom of whatever nonsense your uncle was up to," Leo asked, "or do you want to let it go?"

James raised his eyebrows. "It's a funny business," he said tentatively. He didn't know whether he wanted to get to the bottom of it, as Leo put it. His instinct was to insist that his uncle must have been mistaken, and that Rose had died exactly the way everyone assumed she did.

He thought that he would have told Leo precisely that if not for how this was Sir Anthony's stance, and James didn't care to agree with that man.

And so, driven mostly by a rare and uncharacteristic bout of contrariness, James examined his preconceptions. He wondered how much of his certainty about Rose's fate was due to his reluctance to talk about things that he thought were better left alone. Sometimes it was a kindness to let unpleasant things rest, but sometimes silence transformed an ordinary event into something darker, something taboo.

He thought of his father, and how even now, so many years later, people hesitated to so much as mention his name. People even hesitated to mention suicide around James, as if he might have otherwise forgot how he lost his father. And that only made the loss into something shameful and confusing and which he still struggled now to understand.

Leo's eyes were open now and he was regarding James with a steady intensity that made James want to look away. "What do you think?" James asked. "You're the expert in secrets."

"I don't like it one bit." Leo ran a hand over the stubble on his jaw. "But you were there, weren't you," he said in a non sequitur that James didn't understand.

"The day Rose disappeared. Yes, but I don't remember much of anything," James said.

Leo raised an eyebrow and took a long drink from his glass. "Have you really not seen any of them in twenty years?" he asked after a moment.

"I ran into Camilla a few times and Sir Anthony once," James said. "I never saw Martha or Uncle Rupert because nobody ever asked me back here, and from what I gather they seldom left the place. As for Lilah, I never met her until today."

"Speaking of Miss Marchand, how on earth did you not

think to mention that she was your cousin when we saw her in *Twelfth Night?*"

"Because I didn't know," James protested. "As I said, I never met her, so I never made any connection between Lilian Marchand and Lilah Fairchild. Besides, one hardly expects Bellamys to go on stage."

"Sometimes I forget how very Victorian you are," Leo murmured, but he sounded fond.

"I'm practically bohemian, downright anarchic, compared to this stodgy lot. Can't really imagine any of them allowing a teenaged girl to tread the boards."

"Father did go into conniptions at first," said a voice from the doorway, heavy with amusement. "He can almost stand it when I do Shakespeare, but he was not at all pleased with the cinema. Very common, you see."

James turned to see Lilah. "I didn't mean to eavesdrop," she said, holding up a hand to forestall James's apology. "But I can't possibly go to bed before midnight. It's one of the perils of theater. One gets used to late hours. With film, it's the reverse, of course, and one has to endure catastrophically early calls. But my next film isn't until next month, and it'll be in California, so there's no point in trying to observe what my father calls decent hours."

James performed the calculation that had been bothering him all day. He felt certain that he'd have remembered an infant in residence at Blackthorn, which meant that Lilah had not yet been born the last summer he spent here. Therefore, she couldn't now be over twenty. And yet he felt certain that he had first seen her on screen in the middle of the war.

"You must have been fourteen when you were in your first picture," he said.

46

"Fifteen. I ran away from school." She cracked out a laugh. "I waited until I had got my hands on my birthday money and then I hit the road. There was quite a scene. Father wanted to ship me off to some ghastly school where they lock you in at night."

"I'm surprised he didn't."

"Mother persuaded him that if we forbade me from acting, I'd run off and marry the producer or something equally dreadful."

"Goodness."

"I must say, this has been more diverting than my usual stays at Blackthorn." Still leaning in the doorway, Lilah lit a cigarette and then offered the case to both men, who declined. "I thought father would have an embolism when that sweet old man read the will."

With that, she went directly to the writing desk where Mr. Trevelyan had left the copy of the will and began to page through it. "It's precisely as he said. How disappointing. I was hoping for secret codicils or some indication of what on earth Granddad can have meant by leaving Cousin Martha such a pittance, or any clue as to who Madame Fournier is." She looked up from the papers and wrinkled her nose. "Those clothes. She might as well be wearing a false mustache."

James was faintly shocked by this frankness, but Leo started laughing and Lilah began playing to her audience. "I've spent the evening trying to figure it out," she went on. She's of an age where she could either be Granddad's natural child or a former mistress. But I do know a costume when I see one. Oh, look at this," she said, one fingertip pressed to the paper. "The beneficiary who didn't arrive is a vicar."

Leo hauled himself to his feet and made his way over to the

desk. "Reverend George Foster, vicar of St. Peter's church, King's Lynn," he read from over Lilah's shoulder. "And he was bequeathed the sum of a hundred pounds for the poor box."

"Mr. Trevelyan did mention that there was a missing guest," James said.

"Here's an envelope with your name on it, James," Leo said, tapping the pile of documents on the desk.

Somehow in the confusion following Mr. Trevelyan reading the will, James had neglected to retrieve his own bequest. Now he took the envelope from Leo and slid it into his breast pocket, where he could feel its presence as if it were a weight. He would need privacy in order to look at its contents.

"Was there really an inquest?" Lilah asked. "My father said something about that this evening. I had always been under the impression that Aunt Rose simply disappeared. But tonight everyone was speaking as if she had definitely died. One can't have inquests without a body, can one?"

James glanced at Leo, thinking that if anyone in the room knew the workings of the coroner's court, it should be Leo. But Leo had an abstracted expression on his face as he looked between Lilah and James. "Your father mentioned the police being involved," James said, "but I don't know anything about an inquest."

Everything James knew was secondhand, learned after he had been taken away from Blackthorn and brought unceremoniously to the home of yet another uncle. "I was told that she went for a swim but got caught in a rip tide. She had been in the habit of taking early morning swims that summer." That much was true: he remembered sitting on the rocks, watching her swim out much farther than he was ever allowed. "But I don't think that was anything more than a polite fiction." He was intensely aware of Leo looking at him, something careful and warm in his gaze, and he wished that he wasn't the kind of person who needed to be looked at quite so carefully.

"Evidently, Granddad didn't put much stock in that explanation," said Lilah, still paging through the will. "I suppose it might have been wishful thinking on his part."

Leo frowned doubtfully. "Let's say it's not wishful thinking, though. If your grandfather had reason to believe that Rose's death wasn't what everyone had always assumed, then he must have believed that the truth was important enough to warrant discovery even though he wasn't around to see it."

"Which means," Lilah said, perching on the edge of the desk, "that he probably suspected she was either killed or she ran away and was still alive."

"I think I'm mostly disturbed by the idea that for all those years, your grandfather had doubts," James said. "Do you think he kept it to himself? Has Martha or your mother ever said anything?"

Lilah gave James an odd look, and for a moment she looked much older and more jaded than she ought to. "They hardly ever mention Aunt Rose."

Rose had such a larger-than-life presence in his childhood that James felt vaguely appalled at the idea that people might pretend she had never existed.

But evidently Rose's existence had been swept under the rug as thoroughly as James's father's had been. It bothered James, the idea that the entirety of a person's life could be wiped away by the manner in which they left it. He was over thirty years old and he knew almost nothing of his father. Aside from the photograph that his uncle had, after all these years, chosen to give him, James had nothing to remember his father by, not even anecdotes that had been passed on to him secondhand. He didn't even know anyone who had known his father—except, he supposed, Martha, Camilla, and Sir Anthony, and they had all excised themselves from his life, or he from theirs.

Leo was looking at him now, not with concern, but with a sort of gentle carefulness that made James need to look away so he didn't blush. "It was all so long ago," James said. "I don't know how we're meant to get to the bottom of it."

"Well, with a little bit of digging we ought to be able to uncover the bare bones of the situation," Leo said, returning to the sofa. "There's no mistaking someone running off with someone getting murdered, not unless somebody went to a great deal of effort. Or so I imagine," he added, making James bite back a smile. "I mean, if a person goes for a swim and drowns, there will be evidence of the swim. There will be people who see her with a towel on the way to the beach, for example. There will be clothing or a towel left on the sand. If she runs away, there will be items missing from their belongings. Nobody runs off empty-handed."

"And murder?" Lilah asked.

The words hung heavily in the air until everyone agreed that it was time to go to bed.

CHAPTER SEVEN

"What's this about?" Leo asked when they were upstairs in James's room. He traced his thumb over the line that had appeared between James's eyebrows. Not one bit did he like the haunted look that kept chasing across James's features.

James settled his hands on Leo's hips and leaned in with a sigh, resting his forehead against Leo's. Some of the tension drained out of his body, as if he had been waiting for this. Leo couldn't resist ducking his head and brushing his lips against James's. It was barely a kiss—Leo knew that once he started kissing James, he wouldn't want to stop, and first they needed to talk.

"Every time we turn a corner," Leo said, his lips moving against the corner of James's mouth, "you're ready to jump out of your skin. Downstairs you looked like you had seen a ghost."

James huffed out a humorless laugh and pulled away. "This place is filled with ghosts. I just didn't expect my father to be one of them." He reached into his inner jacket pocket and pulled out a small envelope, then tossed it on the bed.

Leo paused in loosening his tie and sat on the bed, then

51

picked up the envelope. He raised a questioning eyebrow at James, who only gestured for Leo to go ahead. The envelope itself was old and yellowed but crisp and smooth, as if it had sat in someone's desk for decades before being taken out and used. Across the front, James's first and last name were written in a wavering hand. Leo slid a finger under the flap and unsealed the envelope.

Inside was a single photograph. A young man posed with two women and two little girls. The man wore an old-fashioned morning coat, a top hat, and a rather impressive mustache. The ladies wore the sort of gowns from before the Great War that made women look like they were about to pitch forward. Both the children wore pinafores and a profusion of ribbons. But Leo only spared the ladies and children a cursory glance. His attention was riveted by the gentleman, who looked so much like James that there was no questioning the family connection.

The mattress dipped as James sat by Leo's side, close enough that their thighs touched. Leo automatically put his arm around James's waist, still inwardly thrilling that he was allowed to do that.

"My father," James said unnecessarily.

All Leo knew about James's father was that he had been badly shell shocked during the Great War, was sent to an institution, and took his own life sometime thereafter. He also knew that James's mother had remarried and left the country. This sequence of events had been recounted to Leo in a vague enough way that he was fairly certain James's mother had run off with a man while James's father was still alive. James had subsequently spent his childhood either at school or in the homes of various relations. "He was awfully handsome. The

52

woman on the left is your mother?"

"Yes. The other woman is my father's sister, my aunt Charlotte. The girls are Rose and Camilla."

That evening, Leo had tried to detect a family resemblance between James and Lady Marchand, but beyond dark hair and a general air of patrician well-being, he didn't see any likeness. Between James and Martha there was even less, and between James and Lilah there was none at all.

But this picture of James's parents was an unexpected glimpse at his antecedents. It was like seeing what James could have been in different circumstances. James always had a wary air, lines around his eyes that had been earned by work and worry. This man in the photograph had none of it—not yet, at least. He flipped the photograph over and saw the date: June 1911. The man would lose that carefree quality soon enough.

"After my father was sent to the nursing home," James said, "everybody did their best to pretend he didn't exist. There were never any photographs of him, and certainly nobody mentioned him in my hearing. At the time I thought he had done something terribly shameful. After all, my mother ran off and nobody mentioned her because she *had* done something scandalous. So it all added up—my parents weren't mentioned because they were wicked, and nobody wanted to embarrass me by reminding me of their existence."

As far as Leo cared, it was an unspeakable luxury to be born into a family that could feed and house a child, to parents who had probably loved and wanted a child. To have that memory whisked away by relatives—however well-meaning—seemed to Leo so shortsighted as to be very nearly depraved. When a good many people hadn't any family at all, or who had families that were actively terrible, it seemed a shocking waste.

"How old were you when your father went away?" Leo asked, squeezing James's thigh.

"I'm not certain. I was born during the war, so I suppose he was ill my whole life. I certainly never knew the man in this photograph. When we visited, he didn't really talk."

Without knowing more, Leo couldn't say whether Rupert Bellamy had been motivated by spite or by something else. This photograph that James now regarded as if it were an undetonated grenade might have been meant for James to think of his father in his prime. Or it could be a cruel reminder that James came from what the deceased regarded as bad stock.

At best, it was thoughtless to force James's hand in coming here, confront him with an uncomfortable bit of family history, and then make him think about his cousin's untimely death. Leo did not think very highly of this Rupert Bellamy.

"Do you have any other pictures of your father?"

"My uncle—not Rupert, but the uncle who was the vicar in Wychcomb St. Mary—had a photograph of him in uniform. But most of the family photographs wound up in my aunt's possession, here at Blackthorn." He tapped his aunt's image, then sighed. "I don't want to think about this anymore. How was your trip?"

He said *trip* as if Leo had been on holiday. Leo forced a smile. "It was uneventful."

"Likely story."

"It was fine," Leo insisted.

"Leo. You don't have to give me details. But you needn't lie to me, all right?"

Well, of course Leo needed to lie to James. Some of the truth was classified and the rest was unsavory. And while James knew, in broad terms, what kind of work Leo did, hearing the details might make him finally realize exactly what kind of person Leo was. Perhaps he had allowed some of his dismay to show on his face, because James leaned over and kissed his temple, of all things.

"I know you aren't going to tell me the unvarnished truth, you silly man, but I want you to know that you can tell me whatever you want."

And that only made things worse. It was as if James didn't understand that he had invited into his bed—his home, his life—a person who was the embodiment of the things that woke him up in the night.

"Of course," Leo said, and squeezed James's knee.

"You look exhausted. I can't believe you drove all the way here in that state. You didn't even bring any luggage."

"I knew you'd have packed extra," Leo said absently, and James gave him a strange, soft look.

James slid to the floor, kneeling at Leo's feet to pull off his shoes. "Come now, let's get you undressed. Do you need a bath?"

"I showered at your house. Had to get rid of the blood." James shot him an alarmed look. "Not my blood," Leo said reassuringly. Christ, he had to stop talking.

"Good," said James, and set about taking Leo's clothes off, hanging each item carefully in the wardrobe. This was not a seductive undressing, and Leo needed to fix that immediately.

He grabbed James by the tie and watched in satisfaction as James realized what Leo meant to do. James gave him a look that was equal parts amusement and affection.

"But you're exhausted," James protested.

"Mm-hmm," Leo agreed, and reeled James in for a kiss.

CHAPTER EIGHT

From a professional standpoint, James was adamant that Leo needed sleep. After forty-eight hours awake—and likely longer, because knowing Leo, he had underestimated—it was remarkable that Leo was still standing, let alone coherent. He needed a dark room, uninterrupted quiet, and some nourishing food upon waking.

But Leo wasn't his patient. He was his—lover? Friend? Both designations seemed inadequate, almost coy, when used to describe a person who was becoming the fixed point about which James's world orbited. And right now Leo needed him. Not to fret over him, not to put him to bed, but to—well, to take him to bed.

This was how Leo got when he was done with a mission. James was familiar with this reaction from the war. Some people responded to brushes with death with an urgent need for sex. James did not. James responded to brushes with death with an urgent need for barbiturates or, failing that, a place to quietly panic.

This train of thought was interrupted by Leo's mouth reaching a particularly sensitive part of James's neck. "I missed you," James said, and Leo's only answer was to slide James's braces down his shoulders and start in on his shirt buttons.

"Just so you know," James said a little breathlessly, "I'm viewing this as first aid." Leo shoved James's undershirt up and started mouthing at his collarbone. "Oh Christ—no, don't stop, that feels nice. Anyway, I'm viewing all these encounters as first aid. Because otherwise I couldn't make myself fuck a man who really needs sleep. No, Leo, why did you take your mouth away, damn you?"

Leo kissed him soundly and pushed him backwards onto the bed. "Because I don't care if you view it as first aid or last rites or an arcane ritual. I just need you."

"You have me," James said, the words coming out more earnestly than he had intended. "You have me."

It was wildly frustrating, one of the chief inadequacies of the English language as far as James was concerned, that there were no words to express exactly what James felt about Leo, and what Leo meant to him. *You have me* wasn't nearly enough. The alternatives seemed either trite or florid, and he doubted Leo would appreciate them almost as much as he doubted his ability to deliver them with a straight face.

That left him with no choice but to try and show Leo how he felt, and right now that meant pulling Leo down to the mattress beside him, making quick work of his jumper and shirt, then getting a hand inside his trousers.

Leo hissed his approval and James rolled on top of him, bracing himself on one forearm. He kissed Leo again, trying to keep it slow and soft. He brought one hand up to cup Leo's jaw and felt the other man's pulse in his neck, a steady, reassuring thump. God, it was good to have him back. They had only met a little over two months ago, but James couldn't cast his mind back to a time when he hadn't known what Leo felt like

57

beneath him, when he hadn't memorized the precise shape and feel of Leo's lips against his own.

Now Leo brought a knee up so their hips fit more closely together. James gave an involuntary gasp and pressed down in an automatic search for friction, then groaned when Leo arched up, evidently seeking the same.

He kissed Leo's shoulder and saw the edge of the bruise that he had expected to find there, given how stiff Leo's left side had seemed earlier. "Any other wounds I ought to know about?" he asked.

"That barely even counts as a wound," Leo said, his voice rough. "More of a muscle strain with a bit of decorative coloring, really."

Still, James made a show of kissing his way down Leo's torso as if inspecting him for injuries. Actually, there was no *as if* about it: he was very literally reassuring himself that Leo was in one piece. He shoved Leo's trousers and shorts down and then off and carried on his inspection. No sense in doing things by halves.

"What do you need from me?" James asked.

Leo looked down at him, slightly dazed in a way that made James quite pleased with himself. "You'll be doing all the work, so dealer's choice," he murmured.

James nearly rolled his eyes because when Leo said things like that, he knew what he'd get. When he needed something hard, something with an edge, he asked for it. When he didn't ask—well, he was still asking, but for something else.

He bit Leo's hip, just hard enough to keep Leo from falling asleep on him. Then he shoved both Leo's knees up, kissed the inside of his thigh, and climbed back up his body to take his mouth in another kiss. He thrust his hips, testing the position, seeing how they rubbed together like that. And God, it felt good. Like this, he could kiss Leo senseless until he felt the other man come apart beneath him.

Leo wrapped his legs around James's waist and sighed, like nothing so much as a sleepy, lazy cat. Their kisses fell apart until they were only mouthing hungrily at one another. One of Leo's hands found its way to James's chest and the other held firmly to his hip. James brought his hand up to Leo's mouth; Leo took the hint, licking James's palm. Then James grasped them both in one fist.

"Can you come like this?" James asked.

"Don't stop," Leo said, as if there were any chance of James stopping.

James loved it when they were slow and quiet together, when he could almost believe they had all the time in the world. And he loved when Leo let things unfold like this, unhurried and almost calm. He loved watching Leo's pleasure gradually crest and finally overtake him, loved that he now knew the tightening of Leo's grip and the slight hitch in his breath that meant he was close, loved above all how in these moments, when the two of them were cocooned in pleasure and fondness, the rest of the world receded into soft focus irrelevance.

"James, I—" Leo broke off, biting down on James's shoulder as he came. James found himself, as he often did in these moments, murmuring soft and soothing nonsense into Leo's ear, praise and promises, senseless words of gratitude and affection. When he came it was with Leo's name on his mouth, Leo's callused hands on his overheated skin.

He allowed himself a minute to lie there, collapsed half on top of Leo's body. Then he wet a flannel in the adjoining bathroom and used it to clean Leo off.

"Now go to sleep," James said, kissing Leo's temple.

"You like to take care of me," Leo said.

"If you're only figuring that out now, you must be a terrible spy."

At the corner of Leo's mouth was a tired smile and James had to kiss him there too. He pulled the covers up to Leo's chin and then turned the lamp off before getting himself ready for bed in the dark.

CHAPTER NINE

L eo woke with the depressing awareness that he was someplace new, which was quickly chased away by the discovery that James was beside him.

He reached over James's still-sleeping body to fumble on the bedside table for the wristwatch he knew would be there, in the same way that he knew James's toothbrush would be on the left side of the sink and that he wouldn't eat a bite of breakfast until he had downed an entire cup of tea and got his hands on that morning's newspaper. James did things a certain way, sometimes without even realizing he was doing so. Something in his mind was soothed by the knowledge that his watches and toothbrushes and cups of tea stayed in their proper places.

It was the sort of behavioral tic that in anyone else Leo might have found silly, but he felt fiercely defensive of James's carefully ordered world. He would cheerfully shoot anyone who mislaid James's toothbrush, and was only stopped by the consideration that this would displease James and also cause a great deal of annoyance for both of them.

As he shifted on the bed, he saw that a pillow and a quilt had been artfully arranged on the sofa so as to make it look as if someone had slept there. He also saw that James was buttoned up to the chin in his favorite pajamas.

According to the watch, it was half past eight, which meant he had managed a respectable eight or so hours of sleep. A few years ago, this would have left him feeling fresh as a daisy, regardless of how many nights of sleep he had missed. But now he could easily duck beneath the covers and achieve another eight hours.

Careful not to wake James, he replaced the watch, and in doing so paid attention to the way the muscles on one side of his body seemed composed entirely of bruises.

He was, by his best estimate, nearing thirty years old. And if this was how his body reacted to being in his late twenties, he couldn't imagine how bad things would be in a decade. There were good reasons hardly any field agents were over thirty-five. Granted, few agents survived long enough to discover what kind of toll the job would take on an aging body, but that was not a comforting thought. A year ago, he would have determined to push past whatever limits his body dared to impose on him. But a year ago he had worked for a man he trusted rather than a faceless and slightly bureaucratic MI6.

A year ago he hadn't had James.

His mind and his body were in complete agreement that it was time to quit. But then what would he do? He wasn't fit for any line of honest work, and while he had a bit put aside for a rainy day, it wasn't enough to spend the rest of his life as a man of leisure. Leo was too intimately acquainted with poverty to take lightly the prospect of not having work.

He needed to quit, but first he needed to sort out the next few decades of his life. From this end, thirty seemed terribly young, with too much blank space stretching out before him.

He turned his head to look at James. He could, he supposed, tell James all about these doubts that beset him. But that would only result in James offering him everything from a home to money to promises of devotion. The thought made Leo squeamish; it would be churlish to take advantage of James any more than he already had. It was bad enough that he had effectively made James's home his own during the time he spent in England. It was bad enough that he was letting James—well, love him. There was really no question that James loved him; the fish in the sea and all the mute beasts had that one figured out, and so did Leo. Leo loved him back, which was entirely immaterial.

But the fact remained that James was everything lovely and Leo was quite content to be allowed to exist as one of the satellites orbiting James Sommers, to be allowed to share his meals and his bed, to have James's light shine in some limited way on Leo's shadows.

"I can hear you ruminating," James said groggily, rolling over and dropping an arm across Leo's chest. "Rude." He blindly groped for the watch, found it exactly where he expected it to be, and examined it.

"I wonder if we missed breakfast," Leo mused.

"I wonder if there will even be any breakfast." He stretched and rolled to face Leo. "Yesterday's tea was half a packet of digestive biscuits. Evidently, Mrs. Carrow only does supper."

There was a broad range of possibility between a packet of digestive biscuits and a hot meal prepared by one's cook, and Leo guessed that Martha Dauntsey knew it and had her reasons for the packet of biscuits. "I met Mrs. Carrow last night when I used the telephone in the lodge to make my sham call to my sham sister. Will Carrow is a mechanic who was stationed at a nearby airfield during the war and now is saving up money to buy the garage in town."

"I'm surprised he didn't offer to fix your carburetor straight away."

"Oh, he did, but you see, I found the entire experience of being in a breakdown very alarming and needed strong drink and nourishing food."

James snorted.

"Mrs. Carrow is an artist who makes a living selling watercolors to tourists—seagulls and sailboats and fishermen's cottages, that sort of thing—but the other stuff she had in the lodge was—" Leo hesitated. He didn't know whether art was good or bad, but he knew the difference between tourist tat and something else. "I think it might be something special. In any event, she came to live here after getting bombed out of her lodgings in London and before that had never been in service. Neither of them had. They live in the lodge free of rent in exchange for light work, and viewed your uncle as a sort of pet they were glad to look after."

"I'd like to know why in heaven's name my uncle didn't spring for proper servants. I know it was hard to find help during the war, and it might be even harder now, but surely he could have done something. And why didn't he have the roof repaired or the windows fixed? And why isn't there a single fire—electric or otherwise—to be had in this entire house?" As if to demonstrate the need, he burrowed closer to Leo, bringing the blanket tightly around them.

Leo thought his heart might skip a beat. He ought to be used to this by now. They had spent enough nights together, enough mornings together, that it was no longer practical to count them (it was thirty-two). Surely that was enough time for any reasonable person to get used to being…cuddled, or whatever this was. Leo doubted he had ever been cuddled in his life before he met James. He certainly hadn't known that he wanted any such thing. When James touched him like this, he felt—Christ, he felt safe. And it didn't make any sense. Leo's career—hell, his life—depended on his ability to assess danger and seek safety, and he knew perfectly well that there was no possible peril that James could protect him from with a blanket and a strong forearm.

Leo swallowed and tried to collect himself. "I'd like to know how much was in those bank accounts that are mentioned in the will. I'd like a chance to talk with Lady Marchand, because if anyone knows what her father was thinking, it ought to be her."

"She didn't seem upset when Mr. Trevelyan read the will. Surprised, and maybe slightly offended, but not distressed."

"Is her husband so wealthy that she wouldn't notice extra money and an entire extra house?"

"I don't think Blackthorn is worth much to anyone except Martha, and that's only because she hasn't anywhere else to go, as far as I can tell. As for Sir Anthony, he's a Harley Street doctor, so he isn't hurting for money." There was a tightness in James's voice that made Leo pay attention.

"You don't like him," Leo observed. He pushed some hair off James's forehead.

"Is it that obvious?" James sighed.

It certainly was, which in itself was interesting. James was by no means an accomplished liar, but his manners were unexceptionable; he knew how to deliver whatever falsehoods courtesy required. Last night, though, Leo had noticed James's jaw clench whenever Sir Anthony spoke.

"Why don't you like him?"

James let out a breath and turned his attention to the ceiling. "I went to see him about my battle fatigue or shell shock or whatever you'd like to call it. He's the only psychiatrist whose name I knew, and he's a sort of relation, so I thought it made sense. But I forgot that he attended my father. I'm not sure I had even known, to be honest, considering how young I was at the time."

Leo could imagine that James, nerves shattered and future in ruins, might wish he had a family, and therefore might look for help to someone he thought of as a relation, however old and remote the connection. "What did he say to you?"

"He said that it was no surprise that I was unbalanced after the war, considering how my father reacted. He also said that I ought to go to a nursing home indefinitely, because I have what he called a family history of mental disturbance. He said that two close family members took their own lives and he thought—well, he thought I needed constant supervision."

Leo took a deep breath and let it out through his nose. "Did you?"

"Pardon?"

"Did you need—it's none of my business, but were you thinking of—"

"No, no. It wasn't like that. When I got home from France, I was pretty much the way I am now, only more so."

Leo nodded. James startled easily and seemed to get lost in memories of the war when something happened to remind him of those times. He was hardly the only person in England with that set of symptoms, and unless there was a part of the story that James was leaving out, it was perhaps excessive for Marchand to suggest that James needed to be locked up as a suicide risk.

And yet, Marchand may have been erring on the side of caution. If Marchand had been James's father's doctor, he might not want to lose another Sommers. Leo understood the urge to keep James safe. But still—the doctor had obviously disturbed James.

"I'm sorry that happened," Leo said, judging that James did not now or possibly ever need to hear a defense of his cousin's husband.

"I felt like he was putting ideas in my head," James said. "I hadn't wanted to do away with myself and then he made it seem inevitable. As if I was doomed by a family curse."

That brought Leo up short. "He can go get fucked. I'll go tell him so myself, if you don't mind."

"Maybe wait until we're ready to leave," James said, his cheeks flushing.

Leo loved that James, however civilized he was, liked the reminder that Leo was ready to be very uncivilized indeed on his behalf.

James was silent for a moment. "I ought to be more generous about Sir Anthony. It's awful to lose a patient, and to have lost my father and then Rose in quick succession must have been awful."

Something about James's phrasing didn't sound right. "Was Rose Sir Anthony's patient?"

James frowned. "It's funny you ask. No. I don't think so, at least. You know, he used to tell Rose that she needed a doctor. At the time I assumed she had a headache or an upset stomach or something, because at the time I always had one or the other." He paused, and Leo wondered if it was dawning on James that his childhood stomachaches and headaches might have been part and parcel of the anxieties that troubled him now. "But maybe Sir Anthony had noticed that Rose...wasn't doing very well. Even if Rose wasn't his patient, he must have felt responsible. No wonder he was peculiar during my consultation."

Leo didn't point out that James's conclusion only made sense if Sir Anthony Marchand really believed that Rose Bellamy had taken her own life. Leo was certain that someone in this house either shared Rupert Bellamy's suspicions or knew more than they were letting on, and that person might well be Marchand.

"We ought to get out of bed," Leo said. "But first, will you tell me what you think happened to your cousin?"

James was silent for a long moment. "I don't know. One morning Rose simply wasn't there, and the house was in an uproar looking for her. And then my uncle—not Rupert, but Reverend Sommers—drove down from Wychcomb St. Mary to take me back to the vicarage. Later on, people said that Rose had a swimming accident, but—" He paused. "I tried not to think about it. And nobody talked about it, which made it all the easier not to think about."

Leo nodded, taking in this information. There was a lot James wasn't saying. What did he mean by an uproar? Who was there that day? Who summoned Reverend Sommers to take James away, and why? Who were the people who said Rose had a swimming accident? James might not know the answer to any of these questions, but he knew more than he thought. People always did. And Leo was good at weaseling his way into the corners of people's minds.

He shouldn't do that. There was no need to ferret out the Bellamy family secrets. This situation called for sympathy, not espionage. He ought to—pat James's hand, perhaps? Kiss his forehead? He had no clue. He could manage that sort of thing when he was playing a role for a job, but he was trying to be honest—or something resembling honest—with James.

"I wonder if nobody at all talks about her," James went on. "Based on what Lilah said, they don't. And that seems unfair, almost. Unfair to her memory, I suppose. People deserve to be remembered."

Leo clenched his fist. Graveyards were filled with the forgotten. People slipped out of memory as easily as a knife through butter. But not for James. Not for people like James.

"All right," Leo said. "I'll see what I can do."

James raised his eyebrows. "I didn't mean for you to—"

"Let me," Leo said, and forestalled any protest with a kiss. He didn't have much to offer James, but ferreting out secrets was something he could do.

CHAPTER TEN

James entered the dining room to discover Camilla and Lilah grimly inspecting a box of Farmer's Glory.

"It simply won't do," Camilla pronounced, as if personally aggrieved by this box of cereal.

"There was toast, but it went fast," Lilah said. "Good morning, James. Where's your Mr. Page?"

James pulled out a seat for himself. "He's gone to ring the garage." In truth, Leo was prowling about somewhere he shouldn't be. He poured some of the cereal into a bowl and reached for a small pitcher containing milk so skimmed as to be nearly blue.

"It just won't do," Camilla repeated. "When I think of the meals Martha used to organize at Blackthorn, it's hard to believe the same person could put a box of cold cereal on the table and still hold her head up."

"Rationing, Mother," Lilah said, in the tone of someone who had waged this battle a number of times and had little hope of being listened to.

"I sometimes have cold cereal for my own breakfast," James ventured. "Nothing wrong with it."

"Of course not," said Camilla magnanimously. She almost

certainly had never eaten a single spoonful of oat flakes or wheat flakes or any other kind of flakes in her life. "But this is Blackthorn. And Martha's been the mistress of Blackthorn since Mother died."

"You say that as if it's an official position," said Lilah, "like Master of the Horse or Warden of the Bedchamber or—"

"But that's how *she* treated it, darling. She was always very serious about things being done correctly. She and Rose used to get into tremendous rows when Rose tried to sit down to dinner in grease-stained coveralls, or when Rose wandered about the house with a sandwich in one hand. And now here Martha is serving things in packets, the poor dear. It doesn't bear thinking about."

It was the word *coveralls* that did it, or maybe that word combined with the Blackthorn dining room, identical to how it had been in 1927. As clear as if it was happening that moment, he could see Rose leaning against the door frame in a filthy pair of coveralls, carrying a spanner in one hand and eating a tea cake with the other.

"It's my own home," Rose said through a mouthful of cake. *"I'll wear whatever I please."*

Martha looked up from where she was arranging a vase of flowers on a table that was set for twenty. "Consider your sister. If people think she was raised in a home with no standards—"

"Camilla's an heiress. Nobody will care in the least whether she has an eccentric sister. She could have twenty eccentric sisters and people would still be lining up to marry her."

"But—"

"Let it drop, Martha. It's my home. Here, at least, I ought to have some peace."

"Rose—"

"I said let it drop, damn it. If you don't like it, you can take yourself off elsewhere, can't you."

James had been folding napkins, too young for either woman to care whether he overheard their quarrel. Although *quarrel* seemed to be understating the case: the degree of exasperated ire in Martha's voice had been jarring, but even more surprising was the venom with which Rose had delivered that last line. Martha hadn't anywhere else to go, and for Rose to tell her to take herself off was unmistakably cruel.

"That settles it," said Lilah, getting to her feet and startling James from his reverie. "I'm going to assemble a foraging party and see if I can turn up a grapefruit or a packet of crackers."

"They quarreled a lot, didn't they," James said when he and Camilla were alone. "Rose and Martha, I mean."

"Like cats and dogs," Camilla confirmed. "When Martha came to live here, Rose thought herself too old to need looking after. Martha was scandalized by how feral Rose and I had become without a mother, and set about trying to civilize us. So they were rather at cross purposes, you see."

It was hard to imagine anyone more civil than the woman sitting across the dining table, with her straight back and her crisp consonants. James made an encouraging noise and hoped Camilla continued.

"And then there was the question of How Blackthorn Should Be Run," said Camilla, pronouncing the phrase in a way that left no doubt as to its capitalization. "Martha wanted everything just so, as befit the house and its master. Whereas Rose simply wanted to ride her horses and muck about under the bonnets of Father's automobiles. Martha saw to it that there were dinner parties and dances and an endless parade of house parties every summer. Father did love it, of course, playing lord of the manor, but it was Martha's doing."

There was more to it than that, James knew. There were only so many reasons why a widower would entertain on a grand scale, and chief among them was marrying off his children. Based on the argument he had just recalled between Martha and Rose, Camilla's prospects had been at the forefront of Martha's mind, at least. That conversation must have taken place at least a year before Rose died, because Camilla hadn't yet married—and he was sure she was already married that last summer.

And yet, Camilla hadn't made the kind of match that most parents would consider a triumph. At only twenty years old, she had married a doctor over ten years her senior. A psychiatrist, no less, which was the sort of occupation still spoken of in hushed tones and must have only been whispered about twenty years earlier. Anthony Marchand had been a family friend, of sorts, so there was that mitigating factor. And he had gone on to have a distinguished career. But the knighthood and the Harley Street practice had only come after his marriage to Camilla.

James told himself to stop being cynical. It could have been a love match. The fact that there seemed to be no warmth between the couple now didn't mean they hadn't been in love twenty years earlier.

"All this entertaining," James said, dragging his thoughts back to the present. "It all stopped when Rose died?"

Camilla opened her mouth to speak, but hesitated for the briefest moment. "Entirely. Poor Martha," said Camilla. "I think that's what puzzles me most about Father's will."

"How so?" asked James, failing to follow his cousin's change in topic.

"He always looked after Martha. He seemed to even enjoy looking after Martha. They got along better than most married couples, and for more years than most, come to that. For him to leave Martha with hardly enough to live on seems so peculiar, in addition to it being rather cruel to force her to relive that summer."

"She wasn't even his niece, was she?"

"No, she was a third cousin on the Sommers side. Beatrice Sommers married General Dauntsey, who gambled away all his money and hers as well. Martha was their only child."

"Where will she go now? If Blackthorn is to become a home for reformed criminals, where is Martha to live?" James asked.

"I daresay she'll come stay with us in London. Or perhaps she could hire a cottage or a flat." She spoke these last two suggestions with the uncertainty of someone who could not begin to imagine how one went about hiring cottages or flats.

"Maybe she'll come up with a solution for Mr. Trevelyan and keep the house for herself," suggested James.

"Martha? It seems hardly likely that she knows anything."

James wasn't sure if it was his imagination or if Camilla had emphasized *she*, as if to suggest that people other than Martha might be more likely to know what had happened to Rose.

"It seems to me that anyone who cares about Martha's well-being ought to put their heads together and find a solution to present to Mr. Trevelyan, so she won't have to leave her home," James suggested.

"But I don't really know anything. I already told you so," said Camilla. With her fingernail, she shoved a stray flake of cereal around the tablecloth. "It never seemed any of my business." Before James could absorb the idea that Camilla hadn't thought her sister's disappearance was any of her business, Camilla shook her head briskly. "Which is to say that it seemed an unsavory sort of business to dwell on," she said decisively.

Camilla's gaze strayed to the wall over one end of the table, where hung the Gainsborough painting her father had bequeathed to her. It was a landscape, about three feet across, in which sailboats, enormous cows, and wholesome peasants all somehow converged at a stretch of coastline where the sea was as still and sedate as a bathtub.

"It reminds me of Blackthorn," Camilla said, producing a pair of spectacles to better view the painting.

It had been a while since James had seen the shore near Blackthorn, but he certainly didn't remember any cows or peasants or calm waters. In fact, he was pretty sure cows didn't even look like that. He didn't remember pastel hues, either—he remembered rocks and waves and Rose daring him to go further. James didn't see how this gauzy painting could remind anyone of Blackthorn, or, for that matter, anywhere else. "It's a lovely painting," was all he felt capable of venturing with a straight face. "Do you recall who was here the day of the, ah, incident? I'm afraid I was too young to remember. You were there, and so was Sir Anthony. I remember you bringing me tea while the policemen poked about downstairs."

"Tea?" Camilla asked, looking perplexed for the first time that morning.

"I was in my bedroom, and you brought up a tray of tea and biscuits." James had no idea why he had been in his bedroom. Probably to keep him out of the way of the policemen. He remembered peering out the window at the police inspecting the grounds while eating the biscuits Camilla had brought him.

"Oh goodness," Camilla said. "You do have a memory." She

looked at him shrewdly. "Perhaps Father knew what he was about, making sure you were a part of this."

CHAPTER ELEVEN

After seeing James to the dining room, Leo went in search of the telephone. He already knew there was no extension in the drawing room, so the first place he tried was the library. There he found Marchand and the old lawyer. Trevelyan sat at the desk and Marchand paced from one end of the room to the other. Leo slid out of view, concealed by the half-closed door.

"The man had hundreds of thousands of pounds," said Marchand. "And God knows he didn't spend a shilling in the past two decades." He gestured around, presumably indicating the faded curtains and the general state of shabbiness prevailing in Blackthorn. "He didn't entertain. I think I would have heard if he was in the habit of buying racecars or boats."

"I couldn't say," said Trevelyan.

"You mean you won't say," countered Marchand.

"What I *can* say is that the estate comprises five thousand pounds, after all the named bequests have been addressed. That's no mean amount."

"I know that. And I don't need it, of course," he added hastily. "I only want to know what became of the rest. It's my duty."

"I rather think it's my duty."

"If you'll beg my pardon, I think you've been more than a little derelict in your duty in this whole affair. That will!"

"I had nothing to do with the drafting of Rupert's will, although, as I said, it's perfectly valid."

"Who witnessed it?"

"The vicar and his wife."

"Hmph. Rupert was eighty years old, and he drafted this will only a few years ago. Surely, he had previous wills. Did your firm draft any of them, or did you simply leave him to his own devices?"

Mr. Trevelyan hesitated. "He was in the habit of drafting a will every few years and sending it to my office. He wasn't a lawyer, but he was a man of business and perfectly aware of the legal requirements for a binding will."

"He never sent this one to you, though. Why do you think that might have been?" Marchand's tone was barely concealed resentment.

"I'd have thought it was obvious. He didn't want anyone to attempt to persuade him to do something more reasonable."

"And doesn't that tell you that Rupert knew he was behaving madly?"

"What it tells me is that he didn't want to waste his last months having precisely this quarrel. If you'll beg my pardon, Sir Anthony, if you're in urgent need of funds—"

"I'm not in urgent need of anything! It galls me from a professional standpoint to know that my father-in-law was evidently suffering from a severe mental imbalance and nobody saw fit to alert me. Martha didn't, you didn't, the vicar didn't. The man could have been helped."

Leo was surprised to find that Marchand sounded sincere. He probably also wanted the money, but he seemed genuinely distressed to think that old Rupert Bellamy had been suffering.

"There's no evidence that Rupert was anything other than perfectly sane," said the lawyer.

"Ha! That will isn't the product of a sane mind. Besides, with a family history like this one's, I'm inclined to be concerned."

"Family history?" There was a chill in the lawyer's voice.

"I'm speaking of Rose, obviously."

"Rose never left any peculiar wills, as far as I know."

"Damn it, Trevelyan. I mean that she did away with herself, and we both know it."

The lawyer was silent for a long moment. "I know nothing of the sort. There was precious little evidence of suicide at the time, and apparently Rupert was of the same mind."

Nobody spoke, and Leo could imagine Marchand glaring at Trevelyan. "Are you suggesting that someone killed her?"

"I'm not suggesting anything," said Trevelyan in a tone that seemed calculated to irritate Sir Anthony.

Leo judged that this was likely the point at which the conversation began to go in circles, so he knocked on the open door. "I'm sorry for interrupting," he said brightly.

"Who the devil are you?" asked Marchand, whirling around to face Leo.

In the light of day, Leo was surprised to note that Sir Anthony Marchand was—there was unfortunately no denying it—quite attractive, in a broad-shouldered, hale and hearty sort of way. He must have been very appealing indeed twenty years earlier.

"It's Mr. Page, young James's friend," said Trevelyan.

"I was looking for the telephone so I can ring the garage," said Leo.

"Under the stairs," said Sir Anthony, already turning back to Trevelyan.

Leo made his way toward the stairs, where indeed he saw a door that was partly concealed by the paneling. He put his hand on the doorknob when he heard a voice from behind the door.

"It's even barmier than we could have guessed, love." Then a pause. "Yeah, yeah, I did. I told him he had until tonight. Right." The speaker was a woman who had a London accent with the edges sanded off, a low and throaty rumble that suggested a few decades of cigarettes and whiskey. It could have been Lilah, Leo supposed, if Lilah was a very good actress indeed. Camilla was still with James in the dining room, and besides, he doubted that she or Martha could affect this sort of voice or accent. Nor could it be Mrs. Carrow, who spoke with a West Indian lilt, and who would use the telephone in the lodge.

That left Madame Fournier. Well, both he and Lilah had guessed that she wasn't who she seemed to be. The hair, the accent, the clothing—all had seemed a bit too much. But in that case, who was she? And why was she concealing her true identity? Was she afraid of some harm coming to her, or did she plan to harm someone?

CHAPTER TWELVE

When James gave up on his breakfast, leaving half a bowl of soggy cereal and an intractably tight-lipped Camilla at the table, he went upstairs, thinking to grab a jumper before collecting Leo and walking to the village in search of something edible.

At the top of the stairs, he found Martha, standing before a cupboard and attempting to carry a stack of folded bath towels with one arm and a basket with the other.

"Let me take that," James said, reaching for the towels. "No, I insist."

"Thank you, dear. One forgets how much work it is to have a houseful of guests."

"There used to be a veritable army of servants, didn't there? There must have been a dozen."

"More than that, when I first came here. But by the time you started visiting, I think we were down to half a dozen. Three maids, the cook, a gardener, and the chauffeur. That was enough to keep everyone in food and clean bedclothes. We'd bring in more help from the village for large parties. And then there were whatever servants the guests would bring with them, of course."

Martha opened the door to a bathroom and put the used towels into the basket, replacing them from the stack of freshly folded towels James carried.

"Are any of the old servants still in the neighborhood?" James asked. "Perhaps they might remember something." He felt wrong-footed, as gauche as Madame had been last night, but he pushed past the discomfort, remembering that this unpleasant conversation was why they were gathered at Blackthorn in the first place.

But Martha didn't seem bothered. "One of our old cooks married the grocer," she said. "Bridget Halloran, now Mrs. Mudge. None of the rest stayed nearby, as far as I know." They proceeded down the hall into a bedroom that looked like it had been tossed by burglars. Clothing was draped over chairs, cosmetics and mysterious jars littered every flat surface, and damp towels were piled on the floor.

"Lilah's room," Martha explained. "It's like this whenever she visits. I don't know how she achieves this degree of chaos after less than twenty-four hours. If ever a woman required a lady's maid, it's Lilah."

"I can't remember the last time I encountered one of those," James said, straightening one side of the bed covers while Martha took care of the other.

"Nor do I. A pity. Even Camilla fends for herself these days."

That made something occur to James. "She must have had a lady's maid back then, right?"

"There was Greta—no, it was Gladys, Camilla's maid. But I never really knew her. She wasn't a Blackthorn servant. She lived with Camilla and Anthony in London and traveled here with them. She was one of Anthony's girls."

"One of Anthony's girls?" James repeated, trying his best to come up with a non-scandalous interpretation of those words.

"She was from the Society for the Reformation of Young Delinquents. Part of their reformation was apparently training them to go into service."

"This is the charity that Uncle Rupert mentioned in his will, isn't it? I didn't realize that the, er, delinquents were meant to become domestic servants. That seems..." He let his voice trail off, unsure how to delicately phrase his point, but Martha saved him.

"It seems unwise to put pickpockets and shoplifters in among the silver teaspoons and strands of pearls? I was of the same mind. But when Camilla and Anthony first married, they were as poor as church mice. Camilla hadn't turned twenty-one and come into her mother's inheritance, and Rupert wouldn't—well, Rupert was a stubborn man."

"Did he not approve of Sir Anthony?" James asked before he could think too much about whether this question was in poor taste. "I thought Sir Anthony was a sort of family friend even before he married Camilla."

"Rupert had high hopes for Camilla, and as much as he respected Anthony as a professional, it was a bit of a letdown."

In the adjoining washroom, they performed the same switching of the towels.

"And what about Rose?" James asked, his thoughts reverting to their earlier conversation about lady's maids and thinking that a lady's maid might know all sorts of secrets.

Martha stilled in the middle of straightening a towel on the bar. "What about Rose?"

"Did she have a lady's maid?"

Martha actually laughed, her face transforming and reminding James that she couldn't yet be fifty. "Rose wouldn't hear of it. On the rare occasions she'd allow me to persuade her to put on a proper gown, she still wouldn't let anything be done to her hair. A lady's maid would have needed danger money." She sighed. "When I think of the way we used to go at it hammer and tongs, I'm ashamed of myself. That was years lost to the stupidest of quarrels."

They proceeded into a surprisingly tidy bedroom with a matched set of pale green luggage stacked in the corner and the gown Camilla had worn the previous evening draped across the back of a chair. The bed was already made. "I remember some of that," James admitted, thinking of what he had recollected in the dining room. "But it can't have always been like that between you two."

"Goodness no." Martha briskly exchanged towels in the adjacent washroom. "But some kinds of strife bleed over into everything else." She sighed. "Or maybe that's only in my mind. After twenty years, it's hard to tell memory from regret."

"I think that when someone isn't around anymore, it's hard to stop regret from creeping into memory. At least it is for me. There's always the feeling that I could have done better."

Martha was looking at him oddly and James flushed, realizing he had put some of his neuroses on display for someone who was little more than a stranger. But then he saw that Martha's eyes were a bit watery.

"That's precisely it," she said, and they proceeded to tidy Sir Anthony's austere bedchamber in silence.

Next, they entered James's room, and James tried not to look as if he were paying too much attention to the sofa where Leo had purportedly slept. But Martha was in her own world of memories and fresh towels. "It's odd that none of the Blackthorn servants responded to the legacy. I should have thought the amount would have been enough to tempt them."

"Perhaps Mr. Trevelyan couldn't find their current addresses."

"That must be it. But Mrs. Mudge, the grocer's wife, didn't come, and surely Mr. Trevelyan knew where to find her. I daresay none of them want to be reminded of all that."

They proceeded to the last room in the corridor, which had to be Madame Fournier's. She appeared to have traveled light, as the room bore no sign of occupation other than a well-worn carpet bag sitting beside the bed and a shawl folded on top of the pillow.

"Madame Fournier must be one of the former servants," James pointed out. "Otherwise, why would she be here?"

"I should have thought that I'd recognize any Blackthorn servant, even after all this time. They all answered to me."

By now they had evidently finished their tidying and towel-changing mission, and Martha proceeded toward the back stairs. "At the time, the police questioned them all quite thoroughly. Rather too thoroughly, if you ask me. Two maids gave notice in a single week, one maid ran away, and the chauffeur eloped with a girl from the village."

By now, they'd reached the bottom of the stairs and James followed Martha through a baize door. "I always prided myself on being a decent judge of character, but that chauffeur had me utterly bamboozled," Martha said. "I thought he was a decent lad, if rather more handsome than one likes one's chauffeur to be, but evidently he was stringing along a housemaid as well as two different girls in the village. At first the police got very excited, thinking he had perhaps eloped with Rose, but that entire affair was unrelated, it seems."

There was something off about the way she recounted this,

as if she had heard all this secondhand or thirdhand and was merely passing it on. Surely it wasn't only the police who had been hopeful to find Rose with the chauffeur; surely Martha herself must have hoped that her cousin was alive and well and living in sin—unless, of course, she already knew what had become of Rose.

"Martha, what do you think happened to Rose?"

"I wish I knew. I really wish I did, James." She looked silently at him for a moment. "When they told me, I was certain she had only run off, probably to buy a secondhand motorcycle or learn to fly airplanes or something equally trying on one's nerves. But for twenty years to pass without a word from her, she can't possibly still be alive."

Martha had been the de facto housekeeper at Blackthorn, and if anybody had disappeared, she would have known right away. There would have been no question of her needing to be told. Again, James wondered what Martha wasn't saying.

They had reached a small room off the kitchen, a sort of scullery that was now where dirty linens awaited the laundry van, so James placed the basket on the floor near the door. "Who else was here at the time?" James asked, recalling that he never got a straight answer from Camilla. "Did Rose disappear in the middle of a house party?"

Martha's pale eyebrows shot up. "No, there wasn't a house party. Nothing like that. There weren't any guests, unless you consider Camilla and Anthony guests. And you, of course. Naturally, Rupert was there."

James tried to remember whether that summer had been more subdued than the previous ones. If Martha was speaking the truth, then it must have been, without legions of guests, without enormous cars coming and going up the gravel drive, laden with luggage. But none of that had stuck in his mind.

He thanked Martha and watched her leave through the kitchen.

James shoved his hands in his pockets and looked out the window. Not that there was much of a view—there were the withered remnants of a garden and, beyond that, the lodge and the adjacent garage. He could see smoke coming out of the chimney, and suddenly felt chilly in the unheated, empty kitchen.

As he watched, someone emerged from the lodge, a thin figure in trousers, a battered-looking coat, and a flat cap. Carrow leaned against the wall of the lodge in a tense, furtive manner that made James think that either he was sneaking a cigarette or that he was waiting for someone.

Then another figure approached the lodge, coming down the path that led from the side of the house. James stepped closer to the window to get a better look, hoping that he remained unseen by either of the people outside. It was a woman in long skirts and a coat that somehow seemed too short, as if it belonged to somebody else. Beneath her hat, James could see hennaed hair.

At first, he thought that it had to be a coincidence—Madame Fournier surely was not walking to the lodge for the purpose of meeting Carrow. Maybe she was just out for a stroll. Or perhaps she wanted to talk to Mrs. Carrow. Hadn't Leo mentioned that Mrs. Carrow was an artist? Madame Fournier might want to buy a watercolor.

But when Carrow caught sight of Madame Fournier, he moved to the side of the lodge, out of view of most of the house, but still visible from James's window. Madame evidently saw this, and followed him there.

James could hardly believe his eyes, but there was no way to interpret what he saw as anything other than Madame Fournier and Carrow having a secret conversation.

CHAPTER THIRTEEN

A fter discovering that Madame Fournier was in the telephone room, Leo realized two things. First, he would have to wait to use the telephone himself. Second, everyone in the house was accounted for, which made this a prime opportunity to do a little bit of poking about. Nothing excessive, he told himself. Just a peek into everybody's luggage to see if anything was amiss.

A quarter of an hour later, he returned downstairs and found the telephone room empty.

It was a small, windowless room tucked beneath the stairs and made even more claustrophobic by virtue of being paneled in dark wood. He rolled his eyes when he saw that on a little table was an old-fashioned candlestick telephone. The telephone at the lodge was a standard black Bakelite number, but apparently nothing had been done to Blackthorn in twenty years. He picked up the receiver, tapped the switch hook a few times, then gave the operator his number.

A moment later a bored voice was wishing him a good day. At the sound of it he felt a sudden pang of utterly misplaced nostalgia.

"Mrs. Patel! Did you miss me?"

"I spoke to you last night, Mr. Page."

Mrs. Patel had been the latest of a series of agents to serve as secretary, dogsbody, and general right-hand man to Leo's former handler. After their bureau had been absorbed into MI6, Mrs. Patel had been absorbed right along with it, but into a corner of the bureaucracy that Leo had nothing to do with.

"Did you find the information I asked for?" The previous night, Leo had discreetly rung Mrs. Patel from the lodge and asked her to look into a few small matters.

"Your last case had nothing to do with Cornwall," she said instead of answering him.

Leo had long suspected that Mrs. Patel had clearance far above his own and this seemed to prove it. "It's not for work," he confirmed. "It's personal."

"What's personal."

"Ha ha."

"No, I'm being serious. What's personal for someone in your line of work?" She said *your* as if it weren't her line of work, just because she sat behind a desk. "You're not a plumber, fixing a pipe for a friend. Are you on a con?"

"Jesus, no. And shut up. The operator might be listening in."

"Thank you so much for teaching me how to do my job, Mr. Page."

"I have a friend who stands to inherit something substantial if he can figure out a twenty-year-old mystery."

"All right," she said, sounding satisfied. "The body of Rose Bellamy was never recovered. There were no witnesses to her drowning. She was never declared dead."

Leo raised his eyebrows. If Rose had never been declared dead, that meant her money couldn't have been touched. Or at least, so he thought. He supposed rich people had ways of working around the rules. He'd have to look into that. "What about Marchand?"

"Harley Street practice. Rich patients. Two days a week at a private sanatorium in Bedfordshire. He has some kind of stake in the sanatorium. He does all the usual rich people things: splashes out on holidays, sent his daughter to exclusive boarding schools. Daughter is a bit of a hellion—got expelled from one school and then ran off from the second, and now is a darling of stage and screen." She said *darling of stage and screen* in precisely the same flat tone she'd say *Soviet assassin*.

"She's here too. Find anything else on the list of names I gave you?"

"Rupert Bellamy was a banker. Everything very by the book, but he got rich anyway. He married Charlotte Sommers, who was from an old county family that managed to hang on to its money. She died in 1916 of what seems to have been a lingering illness, leaving a packet of money to her daughters, which they came into on their twenty-first birthday." She paused and Leo heard the rustling of papers. "I won't point out that Charlotte Sommers was the aunt of the doctor you met during the passport incident."

Leo sighed. During the case that had first brought him to Wychcomb St. Mary, Leo had resolved matters by giving his passport to a man who needed to flee the country. He still didn't know how Mrs. Patel had found out about it, but a few days later three new passports, all with different identities, had arrived at James's house, wrapped in cheerful paper and tied with a red ribbon. "Now you're just showing off," he said.

She sniffed. "Both Martha Dauntsey's parents died of influenza in 1918. Without a first name, I can't do anything about Madame Fournier."

"Never mind her. It's an alias. Thank you, Mrs. Patel."

Next, he asked the operator to connect him with Little Briars in Wychcomb St. Mary. The phone rang six times before it was answered by a breathless Wendy, the teenaged ward of Edith and Cora.

"Leo!" she cried. "Did you come home only to run off to Cornwall with James?"

"That's about the size of it. Are Edith and Cora about?" Leo had hoped that the elderly ladies might have remembered more gossip about the Bellamy affair.

Wendy let out a sigh. "No 'how are you Wendy?' or 'how are the piglets, Wendy?' Rude."

"How are you, Wendy? How are the piglets, Wendy?"

"Excellent and not quite fat enough to eat. I'll leave you to decide which is me and which is the piglets. I hope James won't mind but I put in a few more garden beds behind his shed."

"It's February. What can he possibly do with more garden—wait. James doesn't have a shed."

"Well, he does now," Wendy said brightly. "Also, there are a few chickens living in it, but they're on the run from the law."

"Wendy, he's been gone for less than a day. How did you build a—you know what? I don't want to know how. It's either black magic or the black market and it's better to keep me in the dark." Wendy had an extremely flexible and communitarian approach to rationing, which involved a steady stream of goods changing hands for what Wendy insisted wasn't technically money or ration tickets. At this point, Leo was pretty sure that subverting the rationing system was the only thing keeping her from running drugs or arms or taking control of the criminal underworld.

"When you get arrested, I shan't do anything about it," he lied.

"Tomatoes, Leonard. Tomatoes and roast chicken."

"That isn't my name, *Gwendolyn*." That *was* her name.

"I bet you miss me terribly," Wendy said.

"Do you know, I really do," Leo said earnestly. It was a little terrifying, how quickly he had let himself get attached to these people. To James's people. They weren't his own—they were borrowed, in the same way that his half of James's bed was borrowed. But they still felt like his own. In reality, Leo didn't have any people and he would do well to remember it.

He wondered, just for a second, what would happen if he disappeared just as comprehensively as Rose Bellamy had done. He had disappeared before, after all. A solid percentage of his jobs ended with him—or the person he was pretending to be—disappearing. Walking away and never coming back was his bread and butter. How long would it take everybody in Wychcomb St. Mary to forget he had ever been there? How long would it take James?

"You needn't sound so cut up about it," Wendy said, breaking into Leo's thoughts. "Anyway, Cora and Edith are at the vicarage. Shall I take a message or do you want to ring them there?"

"Don't bother," Leo said, suddenly eager to end this conversation. "I'll ring again later if I need their help."

CHAPTER FOURTEEN

"I wonder if you'll tell me why you look like the cat who got the cream," James said later, when they were putting on their hats and coats in preparation for a walk that Leo desperately hoped would lead them to a tea shop. He had skipped breakfast, such as it was, and was determined not be done out of lunch. "Where were you off skulking about while I fought to the death over the last teaspoon of milk for my tea?"

"This is slander and calumny," said Leo lightly as he held the door for James to precede him into the garden. "I didn't skulk at all. Not even a little." He was conscious of being pleased that James had guessed what Leo was up to during breakfast, and even more pleased that James didn't seem put off despite his innate distaste for sticking his nose where it didn't belong. "I just took myself on a little tour of the upper stories of the house."

James snorted. "And what did you learn on your tour?"

"Marchand only brought bespoke suits. Not a jumper or cardigan in sight." He gestured between them, demonstrating what normal people wore in the country. Beneath his winter coat, James wore a cream-colored Aran jumper and corduroy trousers. Leo wore one of James's cardigans that always seemed to find its way to Leo's half of the closet and a pair of nondescript brown trousers. They each had on one of the mufflers that Edith knit in such quantity that everyone in Wychcomb St. Mary had at least one. "There's a fine line between being posh and being a pillock."

"Honestly, not that fine a line," James said.

"Even rich people let themselves get a bit rumpled in the country. Otherwise they look even more untrustworthy than usual."

"You just don't like him," said James, smiling a little into his muffler.

"Of course I don't like him," Leo protested. "Anyway. Lilah's room is a tip. Do we know why she's even here this weekend? She wasn't mentioned in the will and Martha didn't have a room prepared."

"She seems close to Martha," James said. "But in that case, you'd expect her to have at least rung ahead."

"Right. Madame Fournier keeps her room as neat as a pin. So does Lady Marchand, surprisingly. A delight to search, both of them. The only interesting item was a carpetbag in Madame's room with the initials GB sewn inside. Of course, she might have bought it secondhand or borrowed it from this GB. But it's still worth noting. Also, she isn't foreign. I'd say East London, but with a pretty convincing effort to sound middle class."

"And that's it?"

They appeared to be alone in the garden, but Leo lowered his voice anyway. "Except for the small matter of a blackmail note that I found in Marchand's bedroom. He was using it as a bookmark, if you can believe it. He's reading *The Eustace Diamonds*, of all things."

95

"I don't care what he's reading!" James said, laughing. "What did the note say?"

Leo recalled the note. It was typed on paper that was thin and slightly gray, but not the cheapest money could buy. "It said 'I'm sure that after twenty years you've got quite comfortable, but remember that there's one other who knows your secret.'" As far as threatening letters went, this was pretty mild. To start with, there was no threat, nor even a demand.

James hummed pensively. "Do you think it was written to Sir Anthony or from him?"

Leo's heart gave a little thrill that James even thought of the latter. In some other world where Leo was able to tell him the details of his job, James might just understand. "The paper was cheaper than what I'd expect from Marchand, but anyone can buy inexpensive paper."

"It might have nothing to do with Rose. He could have received it in London. Although I don't know why he'd bring it with him to Cornwall. I suppose it would be too much to ask for blackmailers to specify exactly what secrets they're referencing."

"Unsporting of them not to, really."

James then proceeded to tell Leo about his conversations with Martha and Camilla.

"So, I'm trying to decide whether gently born young ladies murder one another over failure to wear proper frocks," Leo said.

"Some might, but I don't think Martha does."

Leo didn't think so either, but the animosity between the cousins still made him curious.

They began to make their way down a path that James said would lead toward the village. Neglected garden beds gave way to an expanse of brownish scrub, which in turn led to a low stone wall with a gate that swung open on rusty hinges.

This footpath ran parallel to the shoreline, as best as Leo could tell, but he still hadn't glimpsed so much as an inch of the sea. He could smell it, he could feel the sharp sea breeze, and if he strained he thought he could almost hear it. Hell, he could taste the salt in the air.

"Next time we decide to go to the sea, we ought to do it in the summer," James said.

"And when we aren't investigating a decades-old mystery in a creepy house," Leo suggested.

"Or trying to be civil with family members who were perfectly content to have nothing to do with me for twenty years."

"And who don't have any food in the kitchen despite the house being littered with Meissen porcelain and priceless art," Leo added, and only then realized that James had suggested taking a holiday together. Several months in the future, in fact. It wasn't as if Leo didn't know that James wanted Leo to stick around; it wasn't as if Leo didn't plan to do precisely that.

It was just that hearing James assume this, hearing James speak of a future of shared holidays as if it were a foregone conclusion, made Leo feel appalled with himself. He felt like Mrs. Patel had been on to something when she asked if Leo was running a con.

A path that at first seemed like a shortcut to the village now thinned out to the point of disappearing. "So help me, if this doesn't lead to the village," Leo said, striving for a light tone, "I will eat the first sheep or goat or what have you that crosses our path."

"Not much in the way of goats at Blackthorn, I'm afraid. Nor sheep."

Leo shoved his hands in his pockets and kept his eyes on the path. "Say, you know I'm going to look for any dirt I can find on your family, right?"

If James was brought up short by this sudden change in topic, he didn't let on. "I think that's rather the point of this exercise. If the mystery of Rose's disappearance could be solved without a lot of unpleasantness, it would have been done twenty years ago. Why, did you think I was going to be cross with you for being ungentlemanly or something?"

"There's a difference between unpleasantness that occurred twenty years ago and the knowledge that the person responsible for the unpleasantness is sitting across from you at dinner and a few branches over on the family tree." He scuffed the toe of his shoe along the dirt path. "I'd much rather discover a nonmurderous explanation. I'd rather you have a living cousin than a dead one."

James looked at him oddly. "You expect me to go to pieces."

"I expect you to be slightly miffed that I'm treating your family as murder suspects."

James was silent for a few paces. "Huh. I might have expected to react that way too, if I had thought about it. But I know you and trust you a good deal better than I know or trust this lot."

"Why on earth would you do a thing like that?"

"Don't be daft." James bumped his shoulder against Leo's.

Leo wanted to lay out an itemized list of reasons James shouldn't trust him, and possibly shouldn't trust anybody, but judged it a sad waste of both their time. "That had better be the village up there," he said instead.

It was indeed the village, and high time, because Leo's stomach was rumbling and he was beginning to suspect that he was getting too old to think on an empty stomach.

At the tea shop, they settled into a small table in a shadowy corner.

"So," Leo said when a plate of scones and sandwiches and a scalding hot pot of tea arrived. He had saved this bit of information for when they were sitting face-to-face. "It turns out there was never any inquest. Rose was never declared dead and her body was never found." He gave James a moment to consider this. "That's extremely unusual. Typically, a body washes ashore. You can even predict when and where it will turn up."

"All right," James said slowly. "So she didn't drown?"

"Almost certainly not."

"Either she was killed and"—James swallowed—"disposed of elsewhere, or she didn't die."

The complete picture was a bit more complicated than that, but James had the basic lay of the land and Leo didn't want to muddle things. "Yes. Let's dispense with the low-lying fruit. One, who would have had a motive to kill your cousin? Two, would she have had a reason to run off and let people think she had died? Three, did she seem distressed or disturbed? Afraid? Angry?"

"I don't know," said James, frustrated.

"I know. I know," said Leo, backtracking. "I don't expect you to. Those are just the questions we need to keep in mind as we look for answers." Under the table he pressed his foot against James's. "So," he went on, keeping his voice light and conversational to avoid the impression of interrogating James. "Who was at Blackthorn the day Rose disappeared?"

"Like I said, Martha told me—"

"I know what Martha said. I want to know what you

remember. If you remember anything. And if you don't, that's fine too."

James hummed thoughtfully. "Sir Anthony must have been there when Rose vanished, because I remember him telling me to stay in my room while the police were around. And Camilla brought me tea and biscuits while the police were there. Uncle Rupert and Martha must have been around as well, but I don't remember talking to them. They probably had their hands full with the police."

"Do you remember there being guests?"

"I remember that I got one of the rooms in the guest wing—the room we're staying in now—instead of bunking in one of the tiny attic rooms where children and unattached gentlemen usually stayed. I think Martha was telling the truth about the house being relatively empty that summer."

"How do you know it was that summer in particular that you got that room?"

"Because it looks out onto the tennis courts, and I remember watching the policemen traipse across the court, ruining the lines."

Interesting. Leo would check either the police reports or the newspaper accounts to see if other guests were mentioned.

"Why do you think that the house was empty that summer, when it was usually filled with guests?"

"Well, Camilla had just married Sir Anthony that spring. Maybe there was no point in having all these parties if she had already found a husband."

Leo's eyebrows shot up. "That same year? You're quite certain?"

"I remember because I had to come down from school for the party and missed a cricket match. It was my first year on the team and I was none too pleased about it."

"A cricket match would be when—April at the earliest, right? Lilah was born in August of that year."

James raised his eyebrows. "How can you know that?"

"I went through Miss Marchand's luggage and found her passport."

"Why would Lilah have her passport with her?" James asked.

Leo smiled at the fact that this, not his invasion of Lilah's privacy, was what James asked about. "She also had some French coins in there, so I'd wager she recently returned from a trip. Furthermore, she had about five tubes of lipstick, keys to a car that certainly isn't in the garage at Blackthorn, and about half a pound of hair pins. She does not strike me as a woman of tidy habits. More interestingly, if she was born in August, then her mother was several months into her pregnancy on her wedding day."

"That's hardly unusual."

"It is when you have the sort of grand party that necessitates people coming down from school for the event. That doesn't sound like a rushed wedding. And she must have been very pregnant indeed that summer."

James hummed his agreement. "It just goes to show how unobservant a twelve-year-old boy can be."

Leo thought it suggested something quite different, but he wasn't going to say so. "Well, I daresay there are wedding photographs somewhere in the house. What about Rose? Did Rose have any boyfriends? Or any lovers at all?"

"I was twelve years old, Leo, and I guarantee that I wouldn't have noticed one way or the other."

"You said that Rose taught you to swim and play tennis. What else did she do? Who else did she play tennis with? Camilla?

Martha?"

James furrowed his brow. "I don't remember names. I remember a few faces. A young blond man who made everybody laugh, for example."

"We need to find the picture albums. They have to be around somewhere, because that photograph your uncle left you had paste on the back. It must have been in an album at some point. Speaking of that picture, how close were Camilla and Rose? It looks like they were nearly the same age."

"Rose was a year older. She was twenty-one when she disappeared."

Every time the door to the tea shop opened, a bell rang, and every time the bell rang, Leo casually looked up to catch a glimpse of the newcomer. Now the chime rang, and Leo leaned back so his face would be obscured by shadows.

"Don't turn around," Leo murmured. About half the people in the universe immediately turned when given such an order, but James only calmly buttered a scone.

"Oh?" he asked. "Who is it?"

"Madame Fournier. She's wearing quite a sensible coat. Dark blue," he said approvingly. "And a matching hat."

"What does her coat have to do with it?" James asked.

"I would have thought her the type to wear a cape or maybe something trimmed with cheap fur. Not a dark blue wool single-breasted coat and matching hat. Very smart."

"Leo," laughed James.

The bell chimed again and another woman entered, this time a stranger. She looked around the room once, then again, and seemed on the verge of leaving when she went still, then proceeded across the floor to sit with Madame Fournier. This woman was plump, with rosy cheeks and fair hair that was fading into gray. She wore a brown tweed skirt and coat, a pair of sensible brogues, and worn but respectable fawn gloves.

Leo thought of the little girls in that photograph with James's parents. They both had dark hair, and few people became fairer with age. Unless, of course, they employed peroxide. But the gray at the woman's temples argued against that.

"What are you thinking?" asked James.

"I'm weighing the probability that your cousin ran off and married...a traveling salesman? A grocer?" He eyed the sensible brogues more closely. "A prosperous grocer, at any rate."

"What can you possibly be talking about?" James asked, nudging Leo's foot with his own.

"Madame Fournier is talking to a mysterious stranger. And that, I'll bet, is the first time anyone ever referred to that lady as mysterious. Could Madame Fournier be your cousin? All that makeup and henna could be a disguise."

"I think Camilla and Martha would have recognized her. Besides, I don't think she's tall enough. The Bellamys were always very tall. You've seen Camilla."

"Lilah's rather petite. And so is Martha. Let's see. Who else could be your cousin in disguise?"

"But why *should* anyone be Rose in disguise? Why would she run off and come back twenty years later in disguise? People don't simply run off. People don't disappear."

Leo paused with his cup halfway to his mouth and then gently set it back in the saucer. "People run off all the time. People disappear all the time. *I* disappear. I disappeared yesterday morning, in fact, as far as any of my associates in—in that city will be concerned." The dead Soviet had disappeared too—there probably wasn't a trace of the kid left. Twenty years from now, her family would probably talk about her in much the same way that James spoke of his cousin.

"Your circumstances are different," James protested.

"I ran away from home when I was a good deal younger than your cousin and I never went back. It was years before I dared to go within ten miles of Bristol." He held up his hand to forestall whatever James was going to say. "And people *get* disappeared all the time. But because they're poor, nobody pays attention. Everybody's *used* to poor people disappearing. Maybe they ran off, maybe they went to prison, maybe they got involved with the wrong kind of man. Maybe home was dangerous. Maybe they were—" He lowered his voice. "Maybe they were like us and needed to go someplace new, someplace safe, and knew nobody at home would want to hear about it. We disappear *all the time.*" By the time he finished, he didn't know whether he was talking about poor people or queer people or what. He just knew that the idea of everyone kicking up a fuss about a girl who ran off twenty years earlier was something that only happened when the girl was born with a silver spoon in her mouth.

"I apologize," James said, even though Leo would have bet five quid that he had no idea what he was apologizing for. How could he? For all the horrors he had seen, he was innocent when it came to some things. There was a gulf between them that Leo didn't know how to bridge, or whether James would even want him to.

"Don't worry about it. It's not—" Leo shook his head. "I just want you to understand that whatever happened to your cousin, the only reason it's noteworthy is that she was rich. People don't usually walk away from a rich father without good reason. In any event, I think we can dismiss the idea that she ran off with a man. If she had, she would have turned up before now." Well, unless something had happened to her after running away, but that wasn't worth pointing out.

"It's a pity," James said, "because that's the happiest outcome."

Leo wasn't sure he agreed. There were any number of good reasons to run away. But he understood that James, who had spent his entire childhood being sent away, might not understand this. "We're assuming that your uncle didn't know what happened to Rose. For all we know, the pair of them were in constant communication and he's set you all on this goose chase for one last laugh." He pushed his sandwich crusts around his plate. "So, this afternoon let's visit the Plymouth library to get a look at some moldy old newspapers, then go back to Blackthorn so I can pick up the car."

James furrowed his brow. "Martha will let you stay another night."

"I'm certain she would. But I don't want anyone to look too closely at us." This wasn't the entire truth. Something about this conversation had left him feeling unmoored.

"Leo, we live together." He peered into his teacup. "Don't we?"

Leo swallowed. Denying it would be untrue as well as upsetting to James, but he couldn't agree without feeling like he had committed James to more than he could possibly understand. The fact was that he stayed with James when he was in England. What little he possessed, he kept at James's house. But the idea of sharing a home with James seemed so grossly improbable that he felt like a charlatan saying it aloud.

"All the more reason for us not to be in one another's pockets when we're away from home," he managed. "We don't want anyone to think that I'm anything more than a bachelor friend

105

who stays in your spare room when I'm not traveling for business." Under the table, he pressed his leg against James's.

"All right," James conceded. He looked so disappointed that Leo wanted to crawl into his lap and kiss him.

"Thanks, Jamie," Leo said with a conciliatory smile.

James, his face red, opened his mouth to speak but nothing came out.

"Should I not call you that?" Leo asked. "I just heard your cousin—"

"It's fine," James said quickly. "I like it."

"Good."

"Well, in the interest of getting this done with as soon as possible, instead of going to the library, I ought to go back to Blackthorn and see what I can turn up by way of photographs."

Leo had one item of business to dispatch before getting a taxi to the library, so he said goodbye to James and lingered in his seat in the corner of the tea shop. He waited for Madame Fournier and her friend to settle their bill and leave, then got to his feet and headed for the door, bending once as if to pick something off the ground.

"I beg your pardon," he told a waitress. "But the woman in the mouse-colored felt hat dropped this glove." The glove, in fact, belonged to Wendy, who left stray gloves all over the village. The last time Leo had worn this cardigan, he had found the glove on the edge of the pigsty and rescued it, then forgot all about it. "I don't suppose you know who she is in order to see that it's returned to her?"

"Mrs. Mudge isn't usually so scattered," said the waitress. "And it's a cold day out. She'll be wanting that glove."

"If you tell me where I can find Mrs. Mudge, I can return the glove to her myself and spare you the bother of keeping track of it. Besides," he added, leaning in, "I'm in need of a good deed to do today."

"I'll bet you are," she said with a wink. "Mr. Mudge is the grocer, and Mrs. Mudge will be headed over there now in order to help at the till."

Leo thought about going directly to the grocer, but judged that he'd rather speak with Mrs. Mudge after reviewing the newspaper. He shoved his hands into his pockets and went outside to find a taxi.

CHAPTER FIFTEEN

Upon returning to Blackthorn, James set about scouring the place for photographs. So far, James's search had only turned up a couple of framed portraits of Camilla and Aunt Charlotte in the drawing room, so clearly he had to delve deeper if he wanted useful photographs. He recoiled at the idea of snooping, and felt vaguely anarchic when he dared to carry his search out of the public areas of the house and into his late uncle's bedroom. He hesitated on the threshold, his hand on the doorknob.

He turned the knob and pushed the door open. If anybody didn't like it, they could try to stop him. What was the worst that could happen? They never invited him back? Well, that had already happened and he'd lived to tell the tale.

James had never been in this room before, and his first thought was that whatever restraint and frugality had been shown in decorating the rest of the house were cast aside when it came to furnishing this bedroom. The windows were covered in burgundy velvet, drawn closed to block out all but the most stubborn rays of sunlight. The bed was an enormous four poster, hung with draperies that matched the window curtains. The walls were covered in photographs and prints;

knickknacks and paperweights and God only knew what other horrors were strewn on every available surface. Garishly patterned carpets covered the wood floors. In short, the bedroom of the late Rupert Bellamy contained every Victorian excess James had ever seen and then some.

It was also far and away the most comfortable room in the house. The chair near the bed looked soft and inviting. The acres of velvet, while casting the room into darkness, also kept away any drafts. The art and other objects made the room look like it belonged to someone. This room was somebody's home.

The bedroom looked as if his uncle had merely stepped out. The man had been dead for less than two weeks; it was hardly any wonder that Martha hadn't yet cleared the room out. But he didn't envy her the task—not only because of the sheer volume of work it would involve, but because it would amount to dismantling a life.

Something struck James as off, though. Something was missing or slightly askew, as so much in this house was. He surveyed the room for another long minute before giving up, and turned his attention to the pictures on the wall, which seemed as good a place as any to continue his search.

He immediately found what looked like a professional photograph of Rose and Camilla in pale, gauzy evening gowns with flowers pinned to their bodices and tucked into their hair. They stood before a grand staircase in a house that was not Blackthorn. Based on their ages—they both looked to be in their late teens—he guessed that it was Camilla's debut. He remembered them at this age. He even remembered Camilla wearing gowns of a similar style.

But it was Rose that drew James's eye. This was Rose as

he remembered her—she looked as if she were only barely managing not to laugh. There was something about her expression that made James fancy that she would take off the pretty gown at the first opportunity and proceed to muck about in old clothes she had raided from her father's closet. He doubted those instances had been documented with photographs, though.

He turned his attention to the younger sister. At a distance of over twenty years, Camilla was only barely recognizable. There was the dark hair, the strong jaw, the high cheekbones. She was, James realized, not much older than Lilah was presently, but James had to squint to see even a faint family likeness.

He took the photograph, frame and all, off the wall and tucked it under his arm. He passed over what looked like the wedding portrait of Uncle Rupert and Aunt Charlotte and landed on a photograph of a trio of girls at a picnic. He immediately recognized Rose and Camilla, dressed in pinafores and each carrying a doll. James's gaze slid past the third girl before snapping back. The third girl, a few years older than the sisters, had to be Martha. She was thin and pale then, as she was now, but in youth those qualities had created a delicate sort of loveliness; now they made James want to make sure she had an extra shawl and a cup of beef tea.

He took that photograph too, and then one of Camilla's wedding, feeling all the while like he was committing a bank robbery.

On a low table near the window, half obscured by a vase of dried flowers and a surfeit of lace doilies, James found three photograph albums stacked on top of one another. He sat in the nearest chair and opened one of the albums in his lap.

The photographs dated from about the 1890s—there was a young Rupert, eerily familiar, posed stiffly alongside a younger man James was startled to recognize as his father. Later came a blank spot, where James supposed the portrait that was bequeathed to him had once been affixed. As he turned the pages, the photographs became less posed and the clothing, too, became looser.

Stacking the books beneath the picture frames, he prepared to rise when he saw a teacup on the table beside him. In it was tea—not dried out, but nearly halfway full. When he reached out to touch it, he found that the cup still held some warmth.

Then he realized that the odd quality he had noticed in the room was simply the absence of stuffiness. The room had none of the musty closed-up quality that he associated with rooms that had been unoccupied for even a week. He crossed the room and knelt before the hearth. The ashes were still warm.

He was still on his knees when he heard footsteps in the hall. He swore under his breath and idiotically looked around for a place to hide, before remembering that he wasn't doing anything wrong. He was only trying to solve the mystery that he and everybody else in this house had been asked to solve. Still, that thought did nothing to stop him from feeling like a burglar.

Let it be Lilah, he hoped. Lilah would think it was funny. She'd probably join him.

It was Camilla, yawning and wearing a dressing gown despite it being the middle of the afternoon. She also wore a pair of thick spectacles, and he had a sudden memory of young Camilla surreptitiously pulling spectacles out of her pocket when she needed them, and then just as quickly hiding them away.

"James, darling, what can you be doing down there?" she asked, sounding utterly uninterested in the answer. "Goodness. This room hasn't changed since I was a baby. Oh, you found Father's albums. Full marks to you. Say, you don't happen to have any Seconal, do you? My pill box is empty but I could have sworn I brought enough to last through the weekend. I mentioned it to Anthony and he said you'd be sure to have something."

Oh he had, had he? James tried not to look deeply annoyed. Sir Anthony might only have been suggesting that James, as a doctor, would have sedatives. But Sir Anthony knew from that disastrous consultation that James sometimes took sedatives during his more troubling episodes.

"No," he said. "I'm afraid I don't have any on me." That much was true—he carried a pill box full of his own barbiturates, but they weren't Seconal. He could probably give her the entire contents of his pill case and not notice the difference; he took those pills so seldom that the odds of his needing them this weekend were vanishingly low. The barbiturates James took were widely regarded as harmless, but he wasn't going to start handing them out to people who weren't his patients. "If you need something, I'm sure Sir Anthony could phone the chemist," he suggested.

For reasons he didn't quite like to examine, after he gathered up the photographs, he went directly to his bedroom and reassured himself that his own medicine was exactly where he had left it.

CHAPTER SIXTEEN

When Leo saw Lilah Marchand at the Plymouth library, he wasn't exactly surprised. Visiting the library for archived copies of old newspapers was a natural step to take when investigating something that had happened twenty years earlier. He was rather more surprised that nobody else had thought of it. Unless, of course, they already knew that newspapers from August 1927 would contain no useful information about Rose Bellamy's fate.

He watched Lilah talk to the librarian, but they were speaking too quietly for him to overhear. When the librarian disappeared for a moment, then returned with a large volume which she slid across the desk toward Lilah, he casually approached, his hands in his pockets.

"Miss Marchand," he said, and watched as, for the briefest moment, she startled, then recovered herself so quickly that he might not have noticed if he hadn't been in the habit of watching for just such a thing. She had smoothed over her surprise awfully quickly, but that was because she was an actress, he reminded himself, not because she had something dangerous to hide. Everyone in this mess was a civilian, at least. Nobody in James's cursed family seemed to be spies, high-ranking military officials, members of criminal organizations, government operatives, would-be fascists, or literal Nazis. Just a bunch of hapless amateurs. It ought to feel like a holiday.

"It looks like we've had the same idea," he told her, gallantly unburdening her of the heavy volume that the librarian brought her and simultaneously assuring his own access to whatever material she had deemed worth a trip into Plymouth. A glance at the spine confirmed that it was indeed exactly what he was looking for: a bound volume of the local newspaper dating from August 1927. "Shall we find a table to share?"

"I have a suspicion that you won't hand that book over to me unless I agree." Her voice held very little of the warmth it had the previous night. "Were you following me?"

"Honestly, no," Leo said. "I only thought to get some background information on your aunt's disappearance."

"And what's your interest in all this?"

Before answering, he led the way to a table in a corner of the room where their conversation wouldn't disturb too many other patrons, and held out a chair for her.

"I'm here because James Sommers sewed me up during the war and I'm not going to forget about it anytime soon. If I can help him out with this mess, then I'll do it." This was close enough to the truth that he was in the rare position of hoping he looked sufficiently honest while actually being honest. But Lilah seemed satisfied.

He adjusted the volume so that it sat evenly between them. The musty smell of old newsprint and ink was intense, but not unpleasant. He pulled a small notepad and pencil from his coat pocket and watched as Lilah retrieved the same items from the handbag he had rifled through a few hours earlier.

Leo turned to the evening edition from the second of August.

"Bellamy Heiress Missing," he read aloud, the headline in heavy capitals, the black of its ink only slightly faded by time. "Reward for any information leading to her whereabouts."

Accompanying the article was a photograph of Rose, then one of Blackthorn. In the following days, there were the usual platitudes from various local eminences as well as Rupert Bellamy and Anthony Marchand. Marchand said all the expected things, but at great length, and Leo had the distinct impression that he enjoyed the attention.

Several times the name Stephen Foster was mentioned as a person the police wished to speak to, but who was unavailable due to being hospitalized for an appendectomy. This Mr. Foster was evidently the vicar's son, and described as a close friend of the Bellamy family, with the strong hint of a romance between him and Rose Bellamy. This was the second time Leo had run across the name Foster in connection with this case, and he made a note of it.

Then came a handful of wildly contradictory stories about the chauffeur, various pieces of unsubstantiated gossip, and a photograph of a Blackthorn maid who was also missing. Leo squinted at the photograph, but it was impossible to make out anything more than a small and colorless young woman with fair hair. There was also a photograph of all the Blackthorn servants, each of them little more than a gray-toned humanoid shape. It was too blurry for him to decide whether any of the figures could be Madame Fournier or either of the Carrows, the three people currently at Blackthorn who could plausibly have been employed there twenty years earlier.

But beneath the photographs, a caption named the missing maid as Gladys Button. She was described as a young woman with an unfortunate past: she had been arrested for pickpocketing, but instead of being sent to prison, she was given to the custody of the Society for the Reformation of Young Delinquents, where she had received training to go into service. The article went on to say that the society had been founded five years earlier and that Anthony Marchand was on the board of governors.

Leo also noticed what was absent from all the newspaper accounts: a list of guests who had been present at Blackthorn. Apart from Sir Anthony, Rupert Bellamy, and Mr. Trevelyan, nobody was mentioned by name. He wondered if Martha had been telling James the truth when she said that nobody else had been present that day.

"When do you suppose this photograph was taken?" Lilah asked, indicating the photograph of the Blackthorn servants that accompanied the newspaper article.

The group of servants was posed outside Blackthorn, in a part of the garden Leo recognized from that morning. The low-lying branches of a fruit were visible, all heavy with flowers. "It's spring," Leo said, touching the blossoms in the photographs. "Or early summer, maybe. But it could have been taken the previous year. There might not have been a more recent photograph. Why does it matter?"

"Why are you really here?" Lilah retorted. "And don't tell me that James is keen on inheriting Blackthorn. I can't imagine anybody is, other than Martha. I also can't imagine that James is mean-spirited enough to try to do Martha out of a home."

And wasn't that a curious thing to say. It was true that Blackthorn would need to have a boatload of money sunk into it in order to make it comfortable, and Leo didn't know whether the five thousand pounds in Rupert Bellamy's estate would allow for that sort of expense after death duties were paid.

"It isn't only the house that stands to be won," Leo pointed out. "There's also the money. Besides, you evidently want it at least a little, unless you research old newspapers for fun."

"This is my family history." There was a defensive edge to her words that probably only came through because she was annoyed with him. Why, he wondered again, had Lilah traveled all the way from London?

"It's James's family history as well. He hasn't any other family, you know. And after your aunt disappeared, he was never invited back to Blackthorn. It sounds like nobody ever made an effort to even see him."

Lilah pressed her lips together. "That doesn't surprise me."

"Why not?"

"Because they prefer to ignore unpleasantness. And having James around might have required them to acknowledge that Aunt Rose had ever existed. Children do ask questions."

"The world is filled with people who prefer to ignore unpleasantness, but most of them manage to cope when the alternative is being cruel to an orphan they're actually related to." And it *was* cruelty, the way the Marchands and Rupert Bellamy and even Martha Dauntsey had ignored James. "Are they ordinarily cruel people? You know them better than I do. Was your grandfather ordinarily cruel? Your mother?"

She appeared to consider it. "No. I would have said they weren't. My mother has no spine, though, and will usually go along with whatever my father says."

The implication, Leo noted, was that her father was in fact cruel.

"But Granddad wasn't cruel. I don't know why he never asked James back." She sighed and turned back to the photo-

117

graph in the newspaper. "I'm counting seven servants. What odds do you give that none of them knew anything?"

"Slim to none," Leo said. "One of them had to know. Maybe someone paid them off to keep secret. Maybe someone got them out of the way." He tapped the photograph of the servants, touching first Gladys Button and then the man who had to be the chauffeur.

Lilah raised her eyebrows. "You think someone killed them?"

"The papers keep saying that they ran off, but nobody is saying where they went. You'd think the police would have tracked them down and asked them questions. Hell, you'd think they'd have arrested the chauffeur just for the sake of having somebody to arrest. It makes me think they either did a very good job of disappearing or somebody got rid of them."

"Look at this," Lilah said when they had flipped through a few more pages. "Two days after Rose's disappearance, the paper ran an obituary of Mr. Foster, citing his cause of death as complications from appendicitis."

Leo leaned in. "Evidently, his father was vicar of the church near Blackthorn. If you recall, Foster is the name of the vicar mentioned in your grandfather's will. His death is awfully convenient. The police want to talk to the chauffeur and he disappears. The police want to talk to the vicar's son and he dies. It makes me wonder if anyone else disappeared or died that summer."

"Other than Gladys Button."

"Exactly. Counting Rose, that's four people who left Blackthorn and never returned." It was five, Leo realized, if one included James. He hadn't died or disappeared, but he had been got rid of all the same, and Leo couldn't help but think that it mattered. "Do you think Martha or your parents know anything?" asked Leo, doubtful that he'd get a useful answer but still curious as to how Lilah would respond.

She tapped her varnished fingernails on the tabletop. There was a curious tension in her frame that hadn't been there the previous night. "I think they're all so used to keeping secrets that they hardly know how to go about thinking about the truth, much less telling it."

"I think they all know something, but that they've spent twenty years telling themselves that it's nothing. They're used to ignoring inconsistencies or peculiarities. And this lot don't even talk to one another, so they've never had a chance to compare notes."

Next, they looked at the September newspapers. By September, interest in Rose Bellamy had faded considerably. The police had received dozens of letters from people reporting to have spotted her everywhere from Chicago to Cairo. The paper strongly hinted that rich and eccentric young ladies were liable to run off at the slightest provocation.

It occurred to Leo that he was sitting next to a rich young lady who had herself run away. He read that line aloud and watched Lilah wrinkle her nose.

"Plain misogyny," she said.

"Can't argue with that. But you ran away, didn't you? From school, I believe you said?"

She looked narrowly at him. "Yes. To audition for a role in a film."

Instead he adopted a gentler tone. "How did your father react when you ran away?"

She raised her eyebrows in surprise. "He said he had always expected me to do something disgraceful. What's your point?"

Leo wasn't quite sure, but this case revolved around people

running away, disappearing, not being where they belonged. As always, he wanted to follow every loose thread to the knot at the center, even if it made people uncomfortable. He was about to ask more—had there been trouble at school? Had she wished to upset her parents? How readily had her mother agreed to let her have her way?

But he saw the faintest trace of a resemblance to James in the young woman's face and lost all interest in making her squirm.

CHAPTER SEVENTEEN

T he scent of the grocer—soap and fresh fruit and sawdust—hit Leo like the aroma of a foreign bazaar. He had remarkably little reason to ever enter a grocer's, eating most of his meals either in restaurants or not at all. James had his groceries delivered, except for when mysterious parcels appeared on his doorstep from Wendy. Leo took a moment to notice the slightly too cold temperature, the shelves of inscrutably ordered tins and packets behind the counter, the way people moved with the determination of those who had done the same thing dozens of times and no longer had to think about it.

Behind the counter was the woman he had seen with Madame Fournier at the tea shop, her mouse-colored hat now discarded. According to what James had told him, this woman, Mrs. Mudge, formerly Bridget Halloran, had been the cook at Blackthorn in 1927. He hoped she had a long memory. Gauging how best to approach her, he took off his own hat and adopted his most genial air. "Mrs. Mudge," he said, keeping his voice too low for any shoppers to overhear, but not so low as to invite curiosity. "I'd like to speak with you for a few moments. It's about the Bellamys."

Her posture immediately stiffened and she folded her arms across her stress. "I've nothing to say about them." She had an Irish accent, and spoke with the unease of someone who didn't want to get a friend in trouble. This was how most people reacted when the police or some other authority came around asking questions about someone they cared about or pitied—they didn't want to say anything, but they also weren't prepared to lie. Most people, when forced to choose between lying and informing, became annoyed at having been backed into that corner. He thought he saw a flicker of just that annoyance on Mrs. Mudge's round face, so he changed tack.

"I'm actually wondering if you could help me with something. My name is Leo Page, and I'm a sort of friend of a friend of the Bellamys. You might remember a child, James Sommers, who spent his holidays at Blackthorn."

Whatever she had been expecting, it hadn't been that, because her expression shifted from irritation to bemusement. "Why, yes. Too skinny by half but ate whatever one put before him. A well-mannered boy."

Leo allowed himself to smile. "I'll bet he was. He's a doctor now, and he did a great deal of good in the war. He fixed me up when I was in a tight spot in France, and so I'm trying to help him out a bit now. You've probably heard about Mr. Bellamy's will," he said, guessing that Madame Fournier would have told her all about it over lunch. "The will mentioned everyone who had been a servant at Blackthorn back then. You probably got a letter from the solicitor yourself."

The shuttered expression was back in force. "That I did. I have better things to do, don't I."

"Sensible," he said, although he wondered what might motivate a person to pass up a possible legacy. "No sense borrowing trouble. To be honest, I'm rather worried that this is going to drag up some sordid old stories and cause trouble for people who don't want to be mixed up in it at all, Dr. Sommers included."

She gave a slight nod, so small that she might not have even known she was doing it.

"And he's not the only one who's been dragged into it," Leo went on. He was about to take a gamble. If Madame Fournier really was Gladys Button—and that GB sewn into Madame's luggage was enough for him to bet on—and if after twenty years she was close enough with the former cook at Blackthorn to meet for tea, then maybe Mrs. Mudge had a soft spot for the maid who had run away all those years ago. "There's a housemaid whose name keeps coming up. Gladys Button."

"She wasn't a housemaid," Mrs. Mudge said immediately, as Leo had hoped she would. "She was a lady's maid."

"Ah, I see," Leo said. And that was important, wasn't it? Reformed thief Gladys Button had been elevated to the heights of lady's maid and then dropped into a household of servants who must have been all too willing to turn up their noses at an upstart. She must have been dreadfully unhappy. Small wonder she had run away, with or without the enticement of a handsome chauffeur, and it occurred to Leo that the maid's disappearance might have nothing to do with Rose Bellamy. If another servant had taken Gladys under their wing, that might be the sort of connection both of them would remember twenty years later.

"Alfie!" Mrs. Mudge called to an aproned young man who was rearranging a stack of apples. "You're at the till until I get back."

She led Leo to a storeroom that was even chillier than the

shop. There weren't any chairs, but Mrs. Mudge sat on an overturned crate and Leo followed suit.

"Gladys didn't do anything," Mrs. Mudge said at once. "She was a good girl and not mixed up in any of that sad business, no matter what the papers said, thank you very much. Too biddable by half, mind you, but she was young, and there but for the grace of God. You mustn't bother her. She went through more than enough back then."

None of what this woman had said was proof that Madame was indeed Gladys, which was what Leo most wanted to know. "For her to travel all this distance, though, and after so many years," he said delicately.

"I wouldn't say that Weymouth is such a great distance away," Mrs. Mudge said, and Leo had to suppress a triumphant smile. "I wouldn't have told her about the solicitor's letter if I knew she meant to nip down for the weekend."

That was as much confirmation as he needed that Gladys and Madame Fournier were one and the same, and he judged that pressing for clarification would raise Mrs. Mudge's alarm bells. It was on the tip of his tongue to ask why in heaven's name Gladys had seen fit to arrive at Blackthorn in disguise, but then remembered what he had overheard of Gladys's telephone conversation that morning. *I told him he had until tonight,* she had said. She hadn't come to collect a legacy that Gladys Button might be due, but rather to conduct some other business altogether.

He let the conversation drift back to where it had been a moment earlier. "It was a pity that her name had to be dragged through the papers," he said.

"It was a sin and a shame, what with how grateful she was to even be there. The poor child. She acted as if that lot whisked her off the gallows. Mind you, I wouldn't hire a"—she lowered her voice—"young offender, or whatever they call them these days, but the gentry get their ideas and there's no reasoning with them, is there, begging your pardon. Well, as I said, I wouldn't hire somebody like that myself, but Gladys was a good girl and it was only right to give her a chance, however badly it turned out for her. If she ever did anything untoward, and I'm not saying she did, mind you, it was because someone filled her head with nonsense."

This, Leo gauged, was as close as Mrs. Mudge would come to admitting that she thought Gladys was up to no good—either now or twenty years ago.

"Mrs. Mudge, what do you think happened to Rose?"

"Why, she ran off with the chauffeur, didn't she?" Mrs. Mudge asked, as if Leo were being especially dense. "They put about that story about the drowning to cover it up. She was—well. I'd say she was no better than she ought to be, but she wasn't even that good."

"I see," Leo said. This was the first he'd heard anything of the sort.

Mrs. Mudge hesitated with the dilemma of someone who has good gossip but doesn't want to be seen as the sort of person who spreads gossip. "You could ask anyone," she said, gesturing around as if to encompass the entire village. "The pair of them were shameless, Miss Bellamy and the chauffeur. She was in and out of the lodge at all hours, and the housemaid who collected his washing found Miss Rose's clothes and even—" she lowered her voice "—her underthings right on the floor, where God or anyone could see them."

Leo thanked Mrs. Mudge for her help and began the cold walk back to Blackthorn, his head swimming with possibilities.

CHAPTER EIGHTEEN

J ames spent the remainder of the afternoon in the drawing
room poring over photograph albums. Lilah had returned
from Plymouth in a palpably edgy mood but with a brand
new electric fire, and now the drawing room was, if not
warm, then at least borderline comfortable. Martha sat near
the fire, mending a shapeless garment, and Lilah perched
by the window, smoking a cigarette. Even Sir Anthony was
quiet, reading the newspaper and smoking an endless series
of cigarettes at the desk. Camilla was half asleep on the settee.
Mr. Trevelyan had arrived that afternoon and was next door
in the library. Only Madame Fournier was absent, having
declared herself in need of a rest before dinner.

"I was wondering something," said James, not meeting the
eyes of anyone in the room. "Rose turned twenty-one in
May of 1927. That's when she would have inherited Aunt
Charlotte's fortune, wasn't it?" The Sommers family had been
enormously wealthy; very little of his father's share had made
its way to James, his mother having had expensive tastes and a
penchant for roulette, but Aunt Charlotte's inheritance ought
to have been more or less intact. "Do any of you know what
happened to it?"

He didn't expect an answer. Leo said that Rose hadn't been declared dead, so either that money was still sitting around somewhere or someone in this room had figured out a way to get a hold of it.

"Rather crass to declare people dead just to get money," Camilla murmured sleepily from the sofa. "Father and I were of one mind."

"Quite right," agreed Sir Anthony. "Vulgar."

"Wait. Are you saying she had only just inherited? Only months before she—before whatever happened to her?" Lilah asked. There was a sharpness to her voice that James hadn't heard before. It seemed to surprise Camilla too, because the older woman was now sitting straight, all traces of sleepiness vanished from her face. She looked at her daughter and something seemed to pass between the two women.

"Well, yes," said James, slightly surprised. He had assumed that they all knew this. But Lilah could hardly be expected to know the details of Rose's inheritance if nobody ever spoke of her. "She turned twenty-one that spring. Right after your mother got married."

"Can we find out whether she cashed it all in? All at once? Would the bank still have those records?" Lilah asked. The question seemed to be addressed to the room, but she was looking at her mother, and her mother was returning the gaze.

"You'd have to ask Mr. Trevelyan," said Martha. A wrinkle had appeared on her brow. "He'll be here again for dinner."

Had Mr. Trevelyan known about the state of Rose's finances twenty years ago? Had he, perhaps, had something to do with her missing money? What if Rose had found out? Before James could decide whether these were reasonable suspicions, Sir

Anthony cleared his throat.

"I wonder, James," said Sir Anthony, breaking the quiet, "that you're still practicing medicine, even in such a modest way."

James kept his gaze on the photograph album, which was open to a picture of Camilla in tennis whites. Out of the corner of his eye, he saw that Martha's needle had stilled. "I'm a doctor. It would be a wonder if I didn't practice medicine," he said when he could trust his voice to remain even.

"But—well, it can be a trying profession. When you came to see me in '45, I believe I counseled rest."

Mostly, James was furious that Sir Anthony was doing this in front of Martha and Lilah. "I believe you did," James agreed, flipping the page so he now saw a photograph of Rupert Bellamy and some men James didn't recognize. "But I sought a second opinion." Somewhere behind him, he heard a sound from Lilah that could have either been a laugh or a gasp. "Feeling useful is its own therapy."

James didn't have to look at Sir Anthony to know the man was furious. It radiated off him so James could feel it as surely as he felt the heat from the fire.

"By exposing yourself to situations that bring on your fits, you risk a relapse. You probably heard what happened to Peter Mayhew. Went stark mad after hearing a gun discharge during shooting season. Quite insensible now. Worse than your father ever was."

He wanted to say that he didn't have fits, that he wasn't going to go mad, that he was no longer afraid of turning out how his father did. But there was a glimmer of truth in the poison Sir Anthony tried to pour in his ear. Sometimes a case that was particularly bloody or violent did bring him close to the edge of panic. He would always worry about ending up like his father.

But now he knew those worries were baseless; where another person might lie awake worrying about burglars or housefires, James worried about his mind. The worry would always be there, but he knew it to be far-fetched.

Two years ago, though, he hadn't known. He had fainted while attempting to put in stitches and was terrified that his career as a surgeon—and his life as he knew it—was over. He had been vulnerable and frightened when he sought Sir Anthony's help.

He had spent years thinking that Sir Anthony must have meant well. But now he knew that this wasn't the case. Sir Anthony meant to make him feel as bad as possible. He didn't know why, and at the moment he didn't much care.

"I wonder that you speak so freely about your patients," said James, finally lifting his gaze to look at the darkened countenance of Sir Anthony. He got to his feet and tucked the photo albums under his arm. "I also wonder if my father might have fared better with a different course of treatment."

That parting shot might have been unfair, but James was beyond caring. He needed fresh air. He stowed the albums on top of the wardrobe in his bedroom, out of sight, and decided not to think too much about why he thought this precaution was necessary. He grabbed his coat out of the wardrobe and went downstairs, then stepped outside just in time to see Leo walking down the drive.

"Why on earth do you look so surprised?" Leo asked. James supposed his face was just that readable. Or maybe Leo had simply learned to read it.

"Not surprised, just pleased to see you," James said in a wild understatement. But the truth was that James was always a

129

bit surprised when Leo returned. Not because he didn't trust Leo or because he thought Leo didn't care enough for him to come back, but because it seemed completely fantastical that a person like Leo came to James not only once, not only twice, but again and again. It was as if some rare bird had alighted on James's finger—it would be mad to expect it to become a regular occurrence. "I'm delighted, if we're honest."

Leo gave him a startled *we're in public* look even though James's voice had been pitched low, and even though a heated homosexual affair on the front steps would be the least peculiar thing to have occurred at Blackthorn in the past twenty-four hours.

"Do you fancy a walk?" James asked, shoving his hands in his pockets so he didn't accidentally touch Leo.

"I would indeed," Leo responded, in a tone suggesting that he understood exactly what James meant by a walk.

While James buttoned his coat and put on his gloves, Leo watched him, as if making sure he did up all the buttons properly, as if he wanted to check for himself that James was sufficiently bundled up. The thought made James's heart squeeze in his chest.

As they walked, they told one another what they had learned that afternoon. James told Leo about what he had seen in the photographs and his uncle's bedroom. He told Leo what Sir Anthony Marchand had said to him, and Leo had responded with a gratifying string of profanities and darkly glinting eyes. Leo in turn told James about the contents of the newspaper, his talk with the grocer's wife, and his certainty that Madame Fournier was in fact Camilla's former lady's maid, who had disappeared from Blackthorn at around the same time as Rose.

"In short, you probably flirted with everyone from the owner of a tea shop to an elderly librarian—" James began.

"—and I hardly learned enough to fill a calling card," Leo lamented.

James had seen Leo gently pry information from people, and it wasn't exactly flirting, but it wasn't far from that either. "What do spies do when they're less accomplished flirts than you?"

"Must be tedious."

"Is it ever more than flirting?" James had perhaps let himself wonder about this once or twice, or maybe a few dozen times.

"Not really. Not lately, at least. My specialty is rooting out information, and taking people to bed is really not the most expedient way of going about things." He cleared his throat. "Would it bother you?"

"No," James said immediately. It was mostly a lie.

"Liar."

"I mean, to be perfectly frank, I don't want you to…" He made a vague gesture.

"To fuck other people?"

James felt his cheeks heat despite the cold. "I know we never talked about it."

Leo snorted. "Did we have to? I rather thought the latchkey to your house meant—"

"It did." They had never talked about this—about what they were doing together, about what this meant. James didn't have the words for it; he hardly had the emotions for it. All he knew was that when he thought about the future, he wanted it to be with Leo. And now they had just—James was pretty sure they had just promised one another fidelity, and the thought made him feel almost lightheaded with some combination of relief and fear.

"In any event, you don't have to worry about it. As I said, it's not an issue that arises anymore. And even if it did, I have other means at my disposal."

"The flirting, though," James said, and immediately wanted to hide behind his muffler.

"Are you jealous?" asked Leo, with obvious interest.

James took a moment to consider. "Just a little." He paused and adjusted his own muffler, then turned to tighten Leo's. "But it doesn't exactly bother me." Some primitive part of him wanted to lay claim to Leo, wanted to snarl at anyone who got too close to him. That was a mortifying thought; besides, Leo was a flirt by nature and James didn't want him to change. "Leo, I—" He was aware of Leo's gaze on him and knew that whatever he said next had to matter. "I know what we are to one another," he said, and then immediately regretted it when Leo didn't respond. "I mean," he went on, "I know you like me best. Which makes me sound like a petulant child, and I do wish you'd say something or that perhaps a tree would fall on my head to shut me up because—"

Leo pulled him behind a high garden wall and took his face between cold, dry hands. "To say that I like you best may be understating the case." The sun was now low in the sky; they were sheltered from view by the wall and given privacy by the fact that few people would choose to take a stroll on a February evening that was getting progressively colder. "I like you so much that I feel certain you shouldn't allow it. Somebody, at least, ought to stop me."

"That," James said, before brushing his lips across Leo's, "is one of the stupidest things you've ever said."

"I say a lot of stupid things." Leo wrapped his arms around James's neck. "You're just blinded by affection."

There was a question lurking behind Leo's words, but James didn't know what it was. Throughout this whole conversation there had been a current running beneath everything Leo said, some secret meaning that James wasn't subtle enough to grasp or brave enough to ask about. "Am not," he said, speaking the words against Leo's skin, his lips barely touching the corner of Leo's mouth.

Leo leaned closer, trapping James between the stone wall and Leo's chest. The wall was cold and rough but Leo was warm, his heart thudding reassuringly against James's own. He gave James the sort of kiss that was right at home in shadowy secrecy and against rough stone walls—hard and deep and a little filthier than James was expecting. Leo was rather horrifyingly good at this sort of kiss.

"Where are you spending the night?" James asked. "And why can't it be in my bed?"

"Tomorrow we'll be—we'll be back in Wychcomb St. Mary," Leo said, and James had the distinct impression that he had been about to say *home*. He hadn't realized how much he wanted to hear Leo say that word until now. "I don't care if ten uncles leave you cryptic bequests and I don't care if twenty cousins disappear into thin air. I'll cart you away from here even if I have to chloroform you," Leo went on, his voice rough and his breath warm against James's cheek.

Their lips met again, only hungrier. James decided it was a good thing that he was too old and too prudent—not to mention too cold—to take things much further. He slowed the kiss down, letting some of the hunger dissipate, letting the heat become replaced with something less urgent.

"I should go soon," Leo said. "My car is ready. Come up with an excuse to invite me in for supper, though? Mrs. Carrow is making beef stew and I won't stop thinking about it until I've had some."

"I also need to show you the photographs I found," James said. "And we need to talk to Madame—or Gladys, rather," James said.

"Immediately," Leo agreed, but gave James another kiss before heading back to the house.

CHAPTER NINETEEN

I t turned out that they couldn't talk to Gladys right away
because when they walked through the door, Martha
intercepted them.

"You'll need to stay for dinner, if you please, Mr. Page," she
said briskly. "The table is already set for eight. Odd numbers
are so unpleasant, don't you think, with the people on one side
always more squashed than the other?"

"Good heavens," James said after Martha disappeared around
a corner in the direction of the kitchen. "That's the Cousin
Martha I remember. Rather like being visited by a ghost."

Leo was all too aware that he hadn't yet told James his suspicions about Martha's particular reasons for being secretive
about the events of summer 1927. But James was presently
looking warm and pleased, his hair rumpled from the wind
and Leo's fingers, and Leo just didn't have it in him to pierce
his air of cheerful well-being.

"Who was she going to have occupy the eighth chair if I
hadn't come in just then?" Leo asked, hanging his coat and hat
and then James's.

"Hostesses have a list of single gentlemen they can call upon
at the last minute to make up their numbers," James said.

135

"Do they really? I mean, in 1948 and not an Anthony Trollope novel?"

"Some still do. I can rely on one good dinner a month from such an emergency," he added, grinning sheepishly. "Things are much more casual now than they used to be, and nobody worries too much about seating two women next to one another, but old-fashioned ladies do worry about it if they fancy themselves good hostesses."

"And is your cousin a good hostess?" Leo asked, genuinely curious. From what he had seen, Martha Dauntsey was vague, scatter-brained, and distracted. If she had once cared about hospitality, something must have happened to change that. Could the loss of her cousin be enough to explain such a shift?

"She certainly was," James said. "And before you say that a child isn't likely to notice how well a house is kept, I'll remind you that a growing boy certainly notices when there isn't enough food or when dinner is late. And I remember nothing of the sort. There's an entire third story of guest rooms that must be quite uninhabitable in winter but which used to be filled with guests every summer. She kept everything going. Picnics and garden parties and both girls' debuts." He paused at the base of the stairs. "I'm going to put our coats upstairs and get changed," he said, reaching out his hand for Leo's coat.

Before James disappeared up the stairs, he paused for a moment, looking at Leo. He often did this before taking his leave, in that fleeting space of time when a man might kiss a girlfriend or his wife. Leo had grown to look forward to those tiny moments, when somehow James managed to convey in a single glance the easy affection that a kiss on the cheek might do. Nothing passed between them except eye contact—not a touch, not so much as a move to bridge the gap between them.

136

But Leo still felt held close. He felt—God help him—dear and precious, sensations that were so new after only a few months that they felt peculiar, as if he were wearing a new style of hat and wasn't quite sure it suited him.

That was a lie. He didn't care if it suited him. He didn't care how misled James Sommers was to think that Leo could ever be a person who deserved soft, lingering glances or outrageously chaste moments of fondness. He didn't care at all, because he was greedy and grasping and he would just go ahead and add that to his list of sins.

After getting some goddamned control of himself, Leo poked his head into the library and discovered the elderly solicitor shuffling some papers on a large desk.

"Mr. Trevelyan, isn't it? Leo Page."

"Dr. Sommers's friend," the older man said, nodding.

"I was hoping you could help with something that's been troubling me. I'm trying to help Dr. Sommers with this mystery. Can you tell me whether Rose had a will?"

"She did," said Mr. Trevelyan, after only a brief hesitation. "She left everything to Camilla. Their mother left twenty thousand pounds to each of her daughters, held in trust until they turned twenty-one. So when Rose died, Camilla would have inherited Rose's share even though she herself hadn't yet turned twenty-one."

So, Camilla—and by extension Sir Anthony Marchand—were the direct beneficiaries of Rose's death. Leo wondered whether Marchand had been in desperate need of funds in the summer of 1927. Leo would have thought that a man with a father-in-law as wealthy as Rupert Bellamy and twenty thousand pounds coming his way in a year's time had easier ways to acquire money than murdering his sister-in-law, but one never knew.

But Camilla never had inherited Rose's money, because Rose was never declared dead. "Why was Rose never declared dead? Surely, enough time had passed."

"It was unnecessary," the old man said carefully. "It turned out that she had no assets."

"She was still twenty-one when she disappeared. Which means she went through twenty thousand pounds in less than a year? She must have had expensive tastes."

Mr. Trevelyan gave a wry smile. "Not as far as I recall. She might have bought a few horses or automobiles, but that wouldn't even come close to using up her inheritance."

Leo almost laughed at the idea of a horse or car being a trivial expense, but for these people it was, and the lawyer was right that neither expense even came close to explaining what had happened to all that money. Gambling, perhaps, although that would amount to quite a losing spree. Or maybe she paid the money to someone else. There was at least one blackmailer involved in this case, if Sir Anthony Marchand's letter was evidence of anything. Maybe Rose was being blackmailed.

There was also one known thief involved in this case. Maybe Rose withdrew money from the bank and Gladys had helped herself to some of it. Maybe that was why she ran away.

In any event, twenty thousand pounds was a hell of a motive to murder someone. Camilla or Marchand could have done it without realizing that there wasn't any money to be inherited.

He thanked Trevelyan and went upstairs in search of James. The bedroom door was shut, so he knocked, more for the idea of keeping up appearances than anything else.

A moment later James opened the door, looking perplexed. His shirt was half buttoned and his hair askew, as if he had pulled his jumper off over his head and not got around to finding his comb.

"The oddest thing just happened," James said. "I was looking out the window and you knocked on the door and I remembered something."

"Oh?" Leo shut the door and began doing up the rest of James's buttons.

"That morning, Rose didn't knock on my door. I had been having trouble sleeping that summer. I suppose I was a bit unsettled. In any event, I often woke before dawn and wasn't able to go back to sleep."

Leo knew that James's father had died a few months before Rose disappeared; his mother was evidently already out of the picture if James was spending the summers at Blackthorn without her. It was no wonder he had nightmares.

Leo did up the top button of James's shirt and slid his hands to James's shoulders, unwilling to stop touching him.

"Rose knew I wasn't sleeping well," James went on, "and she always knocked on my door as soon as she was out of bed so I'd know I could get up and join her. But she didn't knock on my door that morning."

"What do you mean by join her?"

"If she went for a swim, I'd poke around the beach looking for shells or sea glass. If she was going for a ride, I'd tag along on Camilla's horse. If she was tinkering with one of the car engines, I'd hang well back because they terrified me. Anyway, that day she didn't knock on my door. So she mustn't have gone swimming, and therefore can't have died in a swimming accident. Which we already knew. But the thing is, I told Camilla."

"Oh?"

"When everyone first realized that Rose wasn't anywhere to be found, I told Camilla that Rose mustn't have gone swimming because she hadn't knocked on my door."

"And Camilla knew that Rose was in the habit of taking you with her every morning?"

"Yes. Then, later on, when Camilla brought me my tea, she knocked on my door—"

"Why were you taking tea in your bedroom?"

"So I wouldn't get underfoot of the police, I suppose. Anyway, I asked if she told the police about what I said, and she told me that she had."

"Which is doubtful, because if she had, the police would have wanted to speak with you."

So, Camilla either lied to the police or lied by omission in order to make them think that Rose had a swimming accident. Or, what was equally likely to Leo's thinking, she and Marchand, and maybe Rupert too, had decided to tell the police a simplified version of the truth. People were forever feeding white lies and half-truths to the police, and Leo could hardly blame them; this was the first relatable thing Leo had heard of Camilla and Marchand doing.

James raised his eyebrows. "I didn't even think of that. Anyway, Camilla and probably Anthony must have known all along that Rose didn't die while out on a swim."

Leo thought about how to phrase this as gently as possible. He brushed a strand of hair off James's forehead. "Unless Rose planned to end her life and didn't want you around to witness it, darling." He didn't know where that *darling* came from. He had never said that word before and felt like a pillock saying it now, but he needed James to know that he was cared for in a way that his younger self hadn't been, even if it was by someone like Leo.

CHAPTER TWENTY

"Let's get out of here. We don't need to stay." Leo looked at him in a measured, concerned way, as if he expected James to go to pieces any moment now.

"I'm fine."

"I know you are." Leo stroked his hands down James's arms, soothing and gentle, but James didn't want to be soothed. Or rather, he didn't want to *need* to be soothed. "But you're not happy here, and why should you be? These people—"

James stepped back, out of Leo's reach, and sat on the edge of the bed. "They're my family."

Leo looked a bit stunned by this. "No law saying you need to spend time with them, though."

"I know, I know." He scrubbed his hand over his jaw. "It's not that I feel like I owe them my time."

"You don't owe them the time of day, James."

James weighed his words, because they both knew that Leo didn't have any family at all, not even one that had abandoned him. "It's just that I don't have any other family."

"You want to get to know them."

"No, not that either. There's this empty space where my family ought to be, like when you've taken a book off a shelf and not put it back. And I've gone around for years with this missing book and—I suppose I want to know what's in the book." He lay back on the bed, looking up at the ceiling. "I don't expect it to be anything good, or even anything especially interesting. I just want to know."

"It's your history," Leo murmured.

"Well, if you want to put it like that."

"That's what Lilah said when I ran into her at the library. She said the only reason she was interested in this business was that it was her history."

"She's not close with any of them," James said. It was something he had noticed but not thought much of. She avoided so much as talking to her father, who seemed to return the favor. With Camilla she kept up a sort of cheerful cordiality. She seemed to make more of an effort with Martha, but the older woman didn't seem to know what to say to her. He was struck by the idea that Lilah might have been as lonely inside this family as James was after being cast out from it.

"She ran away," Leo said thoughtfully. "From school."

"Yes, so she said." James felt the mattress dip and knew Leo had sat a few feet away. He was giving James a little space, and just that knowledge made him reach his hand out. Leo immediately took it.

"Her mother let her go through with it. She left school and took up acting—adult roles, mind you. Do you think she lied about her age? Do you think she really was born that summer?"

James couldn't see what Lilah's acting had to do with the matter at hand, but he could tell that Leo's mind was working, so he stared at the ceiling for a bit, following a water stain along the plaster until it faded away. Leo kept hold of his hand, stroking the inside of James's wrist with the pad of his thumb.

When James turned his head, he saw that Leo was otherwise perfectly still, deep in thought. Sometimes James forgot how handsome Leo was, probably because Leo was so many things other than handsome. But it was always such a pleasure to look at him, his glossy dark hair falling over his forehead, the beginnings of a beard darkening his jaw.

All day he had been wearing a pair of trousers and a jumper that belonged to James, and James wondered if Leo knew that James always got a bit of a thrill seeing him in clothing he had borrowed—or outright stolen—from James. They were near enough in size that they could swap clothes without anything fitting badly, although the swapping tended to go in one direction, as Leo seemed to own next to nothing. When he had first arrived in Wychcomb St. Mary, it was with a single valise, and James later learned that Leo was in the habit of acquiring new clothes for each job and discarding them afterwards. That valise had contained almost all Leo's worldly goods. When James questioned this, Leo had mumbled something about it being safer that way, and he hadn't even bothered making it sound like a convincing lie.

That would be all well and good if Leo enjoyed living like that, but he plainly didn't. James had caught him staring at the way his own few garments hung in the wardrobe beside James's, and the expression on his face had been one of an almost shy satisfaction. He always took the same cup for his tea and returned it to the same hook in the kitchen after washing it with a care that sometimes made James's heart ache. When James's elderly neighbors plied Leo with biscuits and regaled him with village gossip, Leo loved it. This was a man who wanted a home, and James didn't think it took a particularly gifted psychoanalyst to figure out that Leo was

144

punishing himself by refusing to let himself have one.

It didn't follow that Leo wanted his home to be with James, even though all signs pointed in that direction. He kept leaving—but he kept coming back. For all the lies he told and all his ease with artifice, he had never pretended not to care for James, not even once.

But James didn't know how to make Leo believe that the house in Wychcomb St. Mary could be his home, could be *their* home, could be the place they kept coming back to, together. He wanted Leo to know that he could have more than half a bed, half a wardrobe, his own special teacup. He wanted Leo to believe that they could have a life, a future, and that they could do it with one another.

He didn't know how to do that, though. He didn't even know if it was possible. Perhaps they could just keep going on the way they were and eventually it would feel settled. James would keep on going like this for as long as Leo kept coming back.

And in the meantime, he'd do what it took to show Leo that he was wanted, that he was special, that he deserved the good things that he meted out to himself in tiny increments.

"How long do you think we have until they expect us at dinner?" James asked Leo, who was in nothing but his trousers and undershirt as he rifled through James's valise, evidently in search of clothing more suitable for dinner.

"Half an hour, give or take." Leo raised an eyebrow. "Why?"

James made a beckoning gesture. "No reason in particular," he said, but Leo was already in his arms, letting himself be pulled down to the bed.

CHAPTER TWENTY-ONE

"We ought to get dressed," James said, making no effort to get out of bed.

"Two more minutes." Under several blankets and with his head resting on James's chest, Leo was warm for the first time in what felt like weeks. He had no urge to return to the cold, even though James was right. Someone could knock on their door at any minute and he'd rather not have to scramble to make himself presentable. He reached an arm out from under the covers and blindly groped for the cigarette case on the bedside table. James got there first and a moment later passed him a lit cigarette.

With a groan, Leo sat up and took the cigarette. "Downstairs they're using a Ming vase as an ashtray but I can't find so much as a lump of coal in this house," he complained.

"Perhaps Martha doesn't have any money? That's the only explanation I can come up with for the state of things."

"The lawyer would have released some of the estate funds for housekeeping. That's standard." At least Leo thought it was standard among people who had both funds and estates.

"Maybe Martha simply didn't want to go to any trouble on this gathering? It's rather hard on her to have to entertain a house full of guests after two decades of being a recluse, only two weeks after her sole companion died."

"She's grieving," Leo mused. "Can we look at those photographs you found?"

They got dressed and neatened up, then sat on the edge of the bed with the album open between them. Leo turned the pages slowly, watching a decade pass before his eyes. There was nothing in the photographs that he hadn't already guessed, but looking at them gave his mind space to assemble what he knew. When he got to the last page, he shut his eyes and thought.

Camilla and Marchand had apparently tried to make it look like Rose had drowned. At the time of Rose's death, Camilla and Marchand might have believed they stood to inherit a small fortune from Rose.

Gladys Button, the thief turned lady's maid, had disappeared at the same time Rose did. Twenty years later, she had traveled to Blackthorn in disguise.

Meanwhile, someone was blackmailing Marchand—or possibly Marchand meant to blackmail someone.

He could arrange those facts into a logical—and ordinary—enough pattern: Gladys knew something about Marchand, possibly the role he played in Rose's death—and meant to profit off it, but used a disguise so no danger would follow her home. That seemed plausible enough.

But that story, however likely, didn't account for all the stray bits of oddness that he had gathered over the past day. There was the question of where Rose's money had gone. There were the circumstances surrounding Lilah's birth. And what had happened to the chauffeur?

Most infuriating of all was the absence of a body. There

would be no satisfying answer to Rose's fate without a body, living or dead.

"I wonder," Leo said, closing the final album, "if you could steer conversation to a few topics this evening."

"I could try."

"It might involve being terribly rude," Leo cautioned, and explained to James what he needed to find out.

James listened attentively as Leo counted off the salient points on his fingers. "Don't try to be sly," Leo cautioned afterwards. He could give James the tools to do this—his own tricks of the trade but adjusted for James's personality and comfort. "Just be cheerfully oblivious and plow through any awkwardness. You'd be amazed how many people will just give in when the alternative is looking like they have something to hide. The goal is bluff good humor."

"You want me to be boorish."

"Not quite, because nothing you say will be rude on the face of it. You're asking things that anyone might ask, but utterly failing to notice that the people you're speaking to are trying to avoid answering."

James nodded. "I can do that."

Out of seemingly nowhere, Leo was beset with a wave of—gratitude, maybe? James trusted him. He trusted Leo enough to risk permanently alienating his only family.

And there was also something else, a fierce satisfaction at being allied with James, at facing this with him, together.

"There's another thing I need you to do," Leo murmured as they descended the stairs. "I want to look around in the library. Can you watch the door for me?"

"I'll hoot like an owl if anyone approaches," James said solemnly.

Leo jabbed him with an elbow. "Just knock on the door like a normal person. I don't much care if anyone sees me going through your uncle's papers. We're *supposed* to be snooping this weekend, even if nobody seems to remember it. Damn it, you're all so polite."

"Disgusting, I know."

"Rather. It's just that if I find anything, I don't want anyone else to follow my lead."

"Why not? I needn't remind you that I don't particularly want to inherit this place, do I?"

Leo rolled his eyes. He knew that. "It's not that. If there's a secret worth burying for twenty years, I'd rather people not know it's been unburied."

The import of this seemed to register with James. "You're worried."

Leo managed to refrain from saying that he didn't know how not to be worried when James was within ten leagues of even the most theoretical danger. "Just a precaution," he said, and James shot him a skeptical look.

In the library, Leo made for the drawers that were of a size to contain files. There weren't many, and Leo judged that the important papers would be at the solicitor's office in Plymouth. But Leo wasn't interested in those. Mr. Trevelyan had said that Rupert Bellamy was in the habit of drafting his own wills and simply sending them to the solicitor. In that case, he might still have drafts of the earlier, outdated documents, retained so he could repeat the same phrasing, or simply to keep a record.

The first drawer contained bills—all paid promptly and in full, Leo noticed. There was a ledger in which household expenses were itemized in a precise feminine hand, from the minor (eight shillings sixpence to the butcher, another four shillings for eggs) to the major (eight pounds for a new boiler). As Leo scanned the columns, he saw what he thought might be a pattern. Little was spent on Blackthorn's upkeep beyond what it would take for two people to live comfortably.

The second drawer contained a checkbook, a stack of banknotes, and little else.

But in the third drawer he found what he was looking for: an entire file holding nothing but Rupert Bellamy's old wills.

The first one dated from 1929 and left all his assets to be divided evenly three ways among Camilla Marchand, Lilah Marchand, and Martha Dauntsey. It was interesting that Lilah, who at that point was a child of two years old, merited her own share even though her mother was alive. The next will was dated from several years later and said much the same thing but with a handful of annuities for servants and contributions to charity.

The 1940 will left everything to Martha Dauntsey, with an annuity for Lilah Marchand, and several pieces of art for Camilla. The 1942 will appeared to be identical to the 1940 will, but with a flat sum to Lilah rather than an annuity.

Outside the library door, he could hear the sounds of people walking toward the dining room. He'd have to hurry. Once more, he flipped through the various iterations of Rupert Bellamy's will and finally noticed something. The 1942 will was missing a page. The signature wasn't there.

CHAPTER TWENTY-TWO

Dinner was, as Leo had promised, a very tasty beef stew, but it was rendered infinitely more palatable by virtue of Leo's presence on the other side of the table. James couldn't talk to him, as they had both the length and breadth of the table between them, but it soothed something within James to know that he was there, in sight, almost within reach. He didn't dare let his gaze travel to that end of the table too often, though, because he was certain all his emotions were written plainly on his face.

"I found a few photograph albums," James said to the table at large. "There's one that's almost entirely the summer of '27. We should all look at it together." He said this brightly, as if suggesting a fun outing, but it fell flat. He drained his wine glass, hoping for enough courage to plunge headfirst into a willful social transgression. "Why aren't there photograph albums of other summers?" he asked. "There were dozens of snapshots from the summer of '27 alone, but only a handful from other years."

"Don't tell me you've forgotten," said Camilla, almost absently. "You weren't *that* young, Jamie."

James shook his head, genuinely confused. "I have no idea

151

what you're talking about."

"You got a little camera for your birthday and brought it down to Blackthorn that year. None of us were safe. You took photos of me coming out of the sea with my hair wet, some of Rose in the chauffeur's overalls, some of Martha—anyway, you were a menace."

As she spoke, James remembered the camera. It had been a Brownie, not a birthday present but a gift from some relation or another, handed awkwardly to him after his father's funeral as if offered as a consolation prize. "Whatever happened to that camera?" he wondered aloud. "I can't remember ever having it after that summer. And how did the photos wind up here at Blackthorn, rather than at school with me?"

"Daddy confiscated the film," Camilla said. "Of *course* he did," she added knowingly.

She spoke as if she and James were in on a secret, but James had been utterly in the dark until Leo had briefed him earlier that evening.

"Are there any pictures of Mother in old-fashioned gowns?" Lilah asked.

"Not in that album," James said. "Oh, but that's probably because you were on the way." Again, a tense silence fell across the table. "I suppose not all women fancy having their picture taken in that condition."

Mr. Trevelyan cleared his throat and seemed about to break the silence, when somebody at the other end of the table knocked over their glass of wine. The glass was either Madame Fournier's or Sir Anthony's, as they both had to scramble to move their plates to avoid the spill.

"Do you think any of your old gowns are still around here somewhere, Mother? In the attic, maybe?" Lilah asked while people at the other end of the table dabbed ineffectually at the spilt wine. It was incredible, James thought, that a group of people who were probably used to dining without servants couldn't manage to feed and clean up after themselves once put in a house like Blackthorn. It was like the place stripped everyone of basic survival skills. The Marchands certainly had servants in London, but surely even they occasionally resorted to mopping up their own spills; certainly he and Leo did. And yet they all sat around watching the spill as if a footman might materialize from fifty years in the past and see to all their needs.

"Possibly," Camilla said vaguely. "Neither Rose's nor mine would fit you, though."

"No, I suppose not," sighed Lilah. "And it's a bother to have old things taken in just for a fancy-dress party. But anything of Cousin Martha's would fit me perfectly," she added, glancing at the other woman.

It took Camilla a moment too long to respond, and James wasn't sure if she was trying to navigate the awkwardness of explaining that Martha had never had fine gowns or wrestling with a greater truth, but decided to cut in with his own question before the conversation got too far off track.

"In several of the photographs there was a man I think I recognized. Blond, rather handsome." It was like pulling teeth, James thought, making these people talk about the one topic they were meant to be thinking of this weekend. He hoped Leo, at the other end of the table, was having better luck, but when James looked over he saw Leo examining that blasted Gainsborough with a peculiar expression. "He must have been around here an awful lot if he was in so many pictures," James said cheerfully. "Here, I brought along a photograph to jog your memory." He passed it to Camilla, who put on her spectacles to examine it.

"Stephen Foster," Martha said, something tired and wistful crossing her face. "He was the vicar's son."

James remembered what Leo had told him of reading Stephen Foster's obituary, but hearing his name spoken by Martha jogged James's memory. "He was your convenient gentleman!" James said, the realization striking him. All eyes at the table turned to him, and he supposed he ought to explain. "Earlier this evening, Martha said something about eight being a better number for a dinner table than seven, and I remembered that most hostesses have a list of gentlemen they call upon to make up numbers. Mr. Foster, the vicar's son, was somebody that Martha used to call upon."

Nobody said anything, which was extremely disconcerting. Instead they all just looked at him. James did his best to pretend he was unaware of having caused any awkwardness.

"Not just for supper," Mr. Trevelyan finally said. "He was around a good deal for several years."

"I remember," James said. "He taught me to make a kite." The memory had come out of nowhere—standing on a cliff's edge with a man and one of the girls. "Was he having a romance with Rose?"

There was another disconcerting silence. Now even Madame Fournier—Gladys—went still, her fork poised halfway to her mouth. Sir Anthony stared at his wife, who in turn regarded Martha out of the corner of her eye. Lilah's eyes were round, and her mouth formed an O, and she stared at some spot over Martha's head. Martha's face was whiter than ever. Again, it was Camilla who spoke. "James, dear, don't you think we'd better—"

To James's surprise, it was Leo who broke in. "What I don't understand is why you're all so convinced that she died," he said in an unnaturally bright tone, as if continuing a conversation that had already been taking place instead of saying something calculated to shock. "As far as I can tell, there's no evidence to suggest that she's dead. No body, no witnesses, no letter, no inquest. Do you all know something that the police and newspapers didn't?"

Everyone stared at him, including James.

"What I don't understand is why nobody seems to care what happened," said James. "For heaven's sake, we need to talk about this if we want to get to the bottom of it."

"I think we can avoid a scene," said Sir Anthony, glaring at James.

"It isn't that we don't care," said Camilla, still wearing her spectacles and looking very owlish, "but it's deeply unfair for Martha to be dragged through this all over again. It was cruel of Father. I never knew him to be cruel."

"Why was it cruel?" asked James, ready to pound the table in his exasperation.

"For heaven's sake," said Martha. "I'm sitting right here. And I'm not being dragged through anything, Camilla. I'm just a cranky old lady who doesn't like having her peace disrupted. It's a bit of a shock, hearing certain names mentioned after all these years, but we've all been through worse. I daresay Rupert had his reasons and we ought to honor them. So, let's do what James suggested and talk about this."

Another silence fell. There were too many damned silences in this house.

"I know it's indelicate, but was Rose, er. Did Rose have a gentleman that was…" James didn't quite know how to finish that question. He could hardly say *paramour*, however committed to frankness he might be.

"Oh no," said Camilla. "There were never any men."

Before James could decide if it was his imagination or if his cousin had emphasized the last word in that sentence, Marchand broke in. "Camilla," he hissed. "I should have thought this was beneath you."

If it hadn't been for Marchand's surly little outburst, James might not have fully realized his cousin's meaning. There weren't any *men*. But that couldn't mean what James thought it meant. And yet, why shouldn't it? The world was filled with queer people. Was it really such an outlandish notion that one of them should be in his family? He tried to put that thought aside for later and return to the conversation Leo had asked him to engineer. "There were rumors about Rose and the chauffeur, weren't there?"

"He was very handsome," said Camilla, "and one couldn't help but notice, of course. But Rose didn't pay him any special attention."

"I remember Rose spending a good deal of time in the garage," said James.

"I rather think she was more interested in engines than she was in John Davis," said Camilla.

"John Davis," repeated Martha, a smile breaking out over her face. "Now there's a name I haven't heard in a while."

"Every housemaid and shopgirl from Looe to Plymouth found a reason to saunter past our garage," said Camilla. "You'd have thought he was Errol Flynn."

Not Errol Flynn, as far as James remembered, but a young, Cornish Clark Gable who was prone to taking off his shirt and working only in a vest and trousers. Small wonder the local female population had been entranced. James certainly had been, and had also been mortified by his own reaction. It was a wonder he hadn't developed a fetish for automotive grease and spent the rest of his youth chasing after sweaty mechanics with charming local accents.

Rose, however, had been immune to the charms of John Davis. James had been in a state of heightened, mortified awareness in that garage, and while he doubted that twelve-year-old boys in the process of discovering they were bent were the best eyewitnesses, he was almost certain that the two of them had indeed been more interested in engines than they had been in one another. That summer marked the beginning of his noticing what it meant when men looked at women—and moreover, when they didn't.

"His entire"—Camilla made an encompassing gesture over her torso and face—"was a breach of the peace." She refilled her wine glass and reached out to fill Martha's.

"John Davis is taking Mabel Parker to the dance," said Martha in a creditable local accent. "That cow."

"John Davis said he likes my hat," said Camilla, whose accent was less convincing but more remarkable in that she had attempted it in the first place.

Martha cackled. "Whoever would have thought his head would be turned by Gladys, of all people."

"Gladys Button!" Camilla exclaimed, with the air of someone who had been searching for a name and had just found it. "No accounting for taste, I suppose." She laughed, loud and bright, and Martha joined her. James was transported back to other meals at this table. Camilla, prim and serious, but spilling over into laughter at the slightest provocation. Martha and Rose quarreling, but with a fond and amused edge, with give and take, the way sisters fight. Laughter that was totally disproportionate to whatever had been said, and was more for the sake of laughter itself.

It was impossible to imagine either of these women killing Rose. James didn't care how many thousands of pounds had been at stake or how many lies Camilla had told the police. He knew Leo would disagree, would say that people were forever killing their nearest and dearest. But he couldn't believe it in this case.

Then Camilla stopped laughing and frowned. "But wait—no, you're wrong, Martha. John Davis didn't run off with Gladys. When the police came, John Davis was already gone. But Gladys was still here—and running around like a chicken with her head cut off because she was convinced they'd arrest her just for sport."

At the other end of the table, Leo turned all his attention to Martha and Camilla. James knew that the timing of Gladys's disappearance was an open question—had she disappeared before or after Rose?

"Then who did he run off with?" asked Martha.

"I never really thought about it. There were too many other things to think about that summer."

"Too right." The two women caught one another's eye and raised their glasses in a wry little toast.

Too many other things to think about. Gladys and the handsome chauffeur were mere footnotes in a story that involved the disappearance of one girl, and—he glanced at Lilah—the arrival of another.

CHAPTER TWENTY-THREE

L eo's pulse thrummed with the familiar thrill of getting close to the truth.

"I've had two glasses of wine and I'm a bit muzzy around the edges, but we all agree my cousin was a lesbian, yes?" James murmured in Leo's ear when they found themselves alone in the hall after everyone left the dining room in favor of the drawing room.

"At least Camilla thought so, and evidently Marchand as well," Leo agreed. What Leo thought more intriguing was that apparently the entire village believed Rose was carrying on a flagrant affair with the chauffeur, but her family was convinced she had a different secret entirely. He wondered if she had attempted to tell them the truth. It hardly bore thinking of. "Christ, but did you see his face? If Camilla had said Rose was a cannibal he couldn't have been more outraged."

James shot him a confused look. "He's hardly the only one to hold that opinion."

"Yes, yes. But your cousin is long dead." Leo entered the cloakroom, found his coat, and put it on. "The scandals of her personal life ought to have long since mellowed into something that can be alluded to at the dinner table. There weren't even any impressionable youngsters at the table who might have been led down the garden path. Lilah's an actress, for heaven's sake. And for the past twenty years everyone has believed that Rose killed herself, something that Marchand himself has alluded to and which surely is even less respectable than lesbianism."

"It all makes me feel a bit sick."

"Hmm?" Leo paused in buttoning his coat and looked at James, concerned.

"The Marchands of the world will always think I'm unfit to be mentioned at the dinner table. Bent. Not quite right in the head. There's hardly any circumstance of my life that can be discussed in polite company."

This wasn't true and they both knew it—James was a perfectly respectable doctor, well-loved by his patients and a fixture in the village. But Leo understood what he meant—these weren't the only things that mattered. Sometimes what mattered were the things you couldn't speak out loud, the things you didn't dare be honest about. "Let me take you home," Leo said. In Wychcomb St. Mary, there were at least a few dinner tables where they were welcome, secrets and all.

"Leo, I—" James started, and it had to be professional instinct that made Leo stop him.

"Don't."

James had been about to say something he couldn't take back—something sentimental, something dangerous. And he shouldn't go around saying that sort of thing, especially not to people like Leo.

Leo squeezed his eyes shut like a complete amateur, and when he opened them, James was looking at him with an expression that wasn't hurt, thank God, but was somehow worse: it was fond. "Shut up about it and don't quarrel with me," Leo said. "We're in the cloakroom."

"I'll tell you again later, then."

Please don't, Leo wanted to say. Instead he unbuttoned his coat and hung it back up. "I'm not leaving. Not yet." *Not with you in this state*, he didn't say. "Let's go into the drawing room and say that you've convinced me to stay for a drink."

"I thought you wanted to talk to the Carrows about Madame while I speak to Camilla. She's rather above par at the moment, so perhaps it's an opportune time to talk about indelicate topics."

Leo wanted to say that the Carrows could wait, that this whole bloody affair could wait if it came to that. But James had a stubbornness about his jaw and a flintiness about his eyes and Leo knew he wasn't going to be deterred. "All right," Leo said, once again putting his coat on. "If you need me, I have a room at the Three Bells in the village. I'll ring you in the morning."

Leo made himself turn and walk out the door and head down the path to the lodge.

Now that Leo wasn't in as much of a hurry as he had been the previous night, he could take a good look at the lodge. It occupied half of what must have been a stable block before it had been turned into a garage. Ivy covered the walls and a garden bed was tucked into what was probably a sunny corner in the summer. Discreetly out of view of the main house hung a clothesline. The lodge had a worn-in comfort that Blackthorn proper lacked.

When he knocked, Carrow himself answered the door.

"Car still giving you grief?" Carrow asked by way of greeting.

"No, not exactly," Leo said. "May I come in and ask you a bit about that lot?" He gestured to the house.

"Can't do that," Carrow said, even as he ushered Leo inside. "Wouldn't want to give you inside information that might let you win the treasure hunt, would I? Fancy a drink? Beer all right?"

Leo said that he'd love a drink and sat where Carrow pointed him, a wooden chair at the kitchen table. "Happily, I'm not in the running. James—Dr. Sommers—is, though, and he's an old friend of mine. I can promise you he doesn't want to win the treasure hunt, as you put it, so much as to find out what happened to his cousin. He was here when she disappeared."

Carrow opened the bottles of beer, his back to Leo. "He must have been a child."

"Yes. And I gather he was fond of Miss Bellamy, and that she was kind to him at a time when he had precious little of that in his life."

Carrow turned to the table and slid a beer across to Leo before taking a seat. This was the first time Leo had seen the man without a cap. The only light in the kitchen came from a lamp on the dresser, but Leo gauged that he was about forty or so, with a mop of dark hair that didn't yet have much in the way of gray. He was old enough to have been an adult in 1927. He could have been the chauffeur, Leo supposed, although it was hard to discern the remnants of movie-star good looks in Carrow's weather-beaten face. He might have been one of the other servants, though.

"And you want to help him out," Carrow said.

Leo nearly delivered his line about James having stitched him up, but instead simply said "Yes."

Carrow nodded, and Leo had the sense he was coming to a decision. Not wanting to put too much pressure on the other man, Leo looked around the lodge.

On the ground floor was a kitchen and sitting room. Off to the side was a door leading to what had to be Mrs. Carrow's studio. Upstairs probably held at least one bedroom. It was a spacious home for a couple, filled with what Leo could only call nice things—vases of dried flowers, some good old furniture, a collection of dishes in a china cabinet. Between the electric fire and the warmth from whatever was baking in the oven, Leo felt warm enough to loosen his muffler.

Leo could see why the Carrows put up with being in the strange space between servant and tenant. "It's a lovely home," Leo said to Carrow.

"Ah, well. That's all Miriam."

"What's that about me?" asked Mrs. Carrow, emerging from the back room in a paint-spattered smock.

"Only that you made the lodge livable."

Leo stood and greeted Mrs. Carrow, who waved him back to his seat. "It was livable before we moved in," she protested.

"Sure, for spiders, maybe."

Leo had the sense that this was a well-worn conversation, and that Carrow often complimented his wife and she often deflected, and that they both did it with love. They looked directly at one another, as if they were alone in the room, alone in the world, with the only person who mattered.

It made something ache in Leo's heart, made him long for something he preferred not to even think about. It made him wonder what it would be like to belong to a person, to belong to a place and a home the way these two belonged to one another, the way they so obviously belonged here.

And he knew that if he told any of this to James, he wouldn't understand why it wasn't possible. Hell, he'd probably think they were well on course to having it themselves. But Leo knew better. It was impossible, and not because they were both men. Well, partly because of that—if anyone caught them looking at one another the way the Carrows were looking at one another presently, they'd wind up publicly shamed at best. But the real reason Leo couldn't ever have anything like this was that he was all wrong for it. Long ago, he'd cast his lot in with knives and shadows and other things that were sharp and dark and cold. In this warm little home, he was an intruder.

He thought of James's house, which was warm and lovely in its own right, and cursed the entire Bellamy family, living and dead, for keeping James and him miles away from it. But even there, Leo was an intruder. Just because he had been invited in—welcomed, even—didn't mean he belonged there. You could invite a snake into your home and that didn't mean it was a good idea.

Not that Leo had any intention of leaving. He was too selfish for that. He wasn't nearly noble enough to walk away.

"Mr. Page is here to talk about Rose Bellamy," Carrow said.

The couple exchanged a look that Leo couldn't decipher.

"I wouldn't object to talking about Miss Bellamy," Leo clarified, "if you have anything to say. But I'm really here to ask about Gladys Button."

There was the tiniest hesitation before Carrow spoke. "Gladys Button?"

"A former maid at Blackthorn. Does the name ring any bells?"

"Can't say that it does."

"Ah, well. It was worth a try. Do you know anything about Madame Fournier? James saw you speaking to her this morning and I wondered if she said anything interesting to you."

"I did speak with the Frenchwoman. And a lot of nonsense she had to say too, she did, all about how she knew me straight away and it wasn't any use hiding from her."

"What do you think she meant by that?"

"Maybe she did know me—I'll be the first to admit that I don't remember every girl I met in my life, begging your pardon, Miriam."

"Who did she think you were?" Leo asked.

"Can't say she was specific about that," said Carrow.

Leo strongly doubted this. There would hardly have been any point in claiming to know Carrow's true identity without saying what that identity was. Unless Madame—Gladys, whoever she was—was just taking potshots.

"Did she want anything from you?" Leo asked.

"No," said Carrow without elaboration.

"Did she say who she was? I mean, did she introduce herself as anything other than Madame Fournier?"

"As Gladys Button, you mean?" Carrow shook his head. "Gladys Button," he repeated, seemingly to himself. "No, she did not."

"What kind of accent did she have?"

"Accent? Oh, I see what you mean. Inside, she came over all foreign. But no, she sounded normal when she talked to me."

Gathering that he wasn't going to get any more from this vein of questioning, Leo sat back in his seat and took a long pull from his beer. "How long have you and Mrs. Carrow lived here?"

"Two years this past October."

"Why Cornwall?"

"It's as good a place as any."

"Better than most, I should think. My flat was bombed while I was overseas," said Leo, lying through his teeth. Strictly speaking, he hadn't kept a flat in London so much as he occasionally stored luggage at one of the vacant flats owned by the agency. That had, in fact, been bombed. "And it turns out that this country is filled with people who've been bombed out of their homes and I couldn't find anywhere to stay, so now I live in James's spare room."

"He's a doctor, isn't he?"

"Yes, in a village at the edge of the Cotswolds in Worcestershire. Wychcomb St. Mary. Disgustingly quaint. I grew up in Bristol," Leo said, again resorting to a half-truth. He had started out life in an orphanage on the border between France and Belgium, then been sent to live with his sister in Bristol, and then lived on the streets of that fair city after his sister died. Shortly thereafter, his old handler had found him and that was that. "So all that picture-postcard Beatrix Potter stuff is a shock to the system."

This was where Carrow ought to volunteer where he grew up, but instead he opened his mouth, shut it, then collected their empty beer bottles and put them aside. Leo knew he was being dismissed.

"I'd like to buy one of your paintings," Leo said to Mrs. Carrow, "if you'll let me."

Manifesting only a little surprise, Mrs. Carrow said that of course she would be glad to sell him a painting, and led him to the studio. Canvases leaned against two of the walls and an easel was set up in the middle of the room. In addition to the large windows on the north side, there was a skylight, dark now, but which in the daylight must make the room bright and almost cheerful.

"The watercolors go for a guinea apiece," she said, gesturing at a row of pretty landscapes. They were neither so small as to seem insignificant nor too large to fit in a suitcase, and were painted in colors that wouldn't look offensively out of place in most homes.

"And what about the oil paintings?" he asked, nodding at a different series of canvases.

"I don't usually sell those."

Leo could see why. These paintings weren't pretty in the least. Some were beautiful—there was a painting of what looked like Dartmoor, and another of an empty airfield. But they weren't the sort of thing you'd hang over the sofa in the front parlor.

There was also a painting of Blackthorn, its absurd Victorian dollhouse aesthetic twisted around so that it seemed to erupt from the ground like a mushroom. It was not a flattering view of the house, there was no question. But it was also somehow... friendly, perhaps? It was not painted by a person who hated the place.

It was painted by a person who saw Blackthorn for what it was—tacky and overwrought but on a domestic scale. It was a home. This was the first time Leo had really thought of the place in that way. People had lived and died there; children had grown up there. Cold and barren as it now was, it might once have been something else.

For a moment, he thought that maybe it was also painted by a person who knew Blackthorn's secrets.

"That's Miriam's haunted house," said Carrow.

Leo raised an eyebrow. "Does Blackthorn have a ghost?"

"No, it's not nearly old enough for that. But Miriam made it look flat spooky."

"You have an overactive imagination," Mrs. Carrow said fondly.

Tacked up on the wall above the painting of Blackthorn was a charcoal sketch, the only portrait Leo had seen in the studio. It was of Carrow in three-quarters profile. Well, it was an attempt at Carrow in three-quarters profile—even in the sketch, it was obvious that the man wanted to turn to see his wife. His lips were slightly parted, as if he were just about to speak and had been hastily silenced by the artist just before he broke the pose. It was a portrait of a man who was dying to look at the woman he loved, and was only holding off out of fondness for her.

The portrait was one of love caught in the act. Love was there in every stroke of charcoal over paper, in the roughly drawn jaw and the slope of his nose.

Placed alongside the painting of Blackthorn, the two images looked like they somehow belonged. Carrow was not, objectively, a handsome man; Blackthorn was not an attractive house. But they had both been captured by a hand that knew them, and saw them for what they were, and didn't seek to change them.

Maybe, also, the subjects of both paintings had secrets they didn't want to give up.

CHAPTER TWENTY-FOUR

J ames would have preferred to talk to Camilla alone, but found her ensconced with Martha by the fire in the drawing room. He pulled a Chippendale chair toward the settee where the cousins sat and prepared to be rude.

"I *am* sorry," he said, sitting down. "I know this is none of my business, but I feel that since we're all still here, we've agreed to tolerate a certain amount of rudeness, don't you think? If we wanted manners, we wouldn't be doing this."

Camilla reached to the floor and retrieved a mostly empty bottle of wine and held it out unsteadily to James, who declined. "I think you must be right. We've all chosen manners for years and years. And that's all to the good—"

"It really isn't," Martha cut in.

"It is, though. It is. There are reasons why one doesn't discuss the unpleasant things. It's because they're unpleasant," Camilla said, with the air of someone making a groundbreaking pronouncement. She was very drunk indeed.

"Can't stand unpleasant things myself," said James, aware that he sounded inane but also that he was being honest. "Or talking about them, at least. Thinking about them either, come to think."

"Good heavens, both of you," said Martha.

"No, no. It's just—we just had a war—"

"*Very* unpleasant!" said Camilla.

"Chock-full of unpleasantness," agreed James. "It does me in when I think too hard about it all or when I'm reminded too abruptly of it. But then the *not* thinking about it becomes the actual unpleasantness, you know?"

"I do not," said Camilla solemnly. "Wine."

"I understand," said Martha, who appeared to be the more sober of the two women. "One spends so much effort not thinking about a thing that it becomes a sort of obsession."

"Like Victorians and ankles," said Camilla. "It becomes a sort of perversion. Or is it a fetish?"

"Yes, exactly!" said James. "One forgets that the thing one's so concerned about is just *ankles*. And I wonder if some things in 1927 are just—"

"Ankles?" asked Camilla, wide-eyed.

"Well, mundane, I suppose. Or straightforward, at least." James was afraid he was speaking in circles, so he took the photographs out of his coat pocket and handed them to the ladies, carefully watching their faces for recognition. One was a photograph of Camilla in an old-fashioned bathing costume. Another was a photograph of Rose in a grimy coverall. Both were from the summer of 1927. Neither woman spoke.

"Of these two women," James said, very quietly, "there's only one who could possibly be pregnant. Lilah was born at most two months after these photographs were taken. I know tall women can conceal pregnancy, but not in a bathing costume."

Camilla and Martha looked at one another, but neither spoke.

"As I said, I know it's none of my concern," James went on. "And you certainly don't owe me any explanation. If you tell me to leave it alone, I will. But did Rose go off to hospital to have Lilah?"

It added up, James thought. Rose could have died giving birth or—and he knew he was being too optimistic, but sometimes there were happy outcomes and it was all right to hold on to that hope—she might have turned the baby over to her sister and gone somewhere new to start fresh, perhaps using the money she had recently inherited and presumably withdrawn from her bank account.

If Rose had managed to conceal the pregnancy from her sister, cousin, and father—and James had known of stranger things happening—she might have gone to the hospital on the morning of August first without any explanation. It wouldn't be so far-fetched to suppose that someone might call the police in those circumstances. Gladys Button and the chauffeur might be totally unrelated.

"No," said Martha. "Rose didn't go off to have Lilah. But I did."

CHAPTER TWENTY-FIVE

That, of course, had been the other possibility, the one that Leo had favored. There had been no full-length photographs of Martha from the summer of 1927 whatsoever.

"You weren't here when Rose disappeared," James said, recalling that Martha had needed to be told of Rose's disappearance, and that she hadn't been mentioned in any of the newspaper reports. "Were you already at the hospital?"

"I left Blackthorn in June, when the situation became too obvious to conceal with cardigans and scarves. We all but closed up the house. I planned to come back after the deed was done."

"Who was the, ah…" James found that there really was a limit to the social gaffes he was willing to make.

But Martha seemed to understand. "Stephen Foster," she said.

"And he, ah, wouldn't do the decent thing?" James winced at his phrasing.

Camilla let out a single *ha!*

"Oh, he would," said Martha. "But I wouldn't. We were badly suited. And Rupert needed me here."

"Did Uncle Rupert know?"

"Of course," Martha said, sounding surprised. "Everyone knew. Well, everyone in the family, at least. I thought *you* knew, James. You were here for part of the summer, after all."

James didn't know how he could have missed such a thing, but then realized that at age twelve he might not have known the difference between a woman who was becoming a bit portly and a woman who was expecting a baby, especially if she was taking care to conceal her shape. "What did you plan on doing with the baby?"

"Adoption," Martha said simply.

"Stephen was furious," Camilla said.

Before James could ask what had happened to result in Camilla and Marchand taking Lilah, the girl herself entered the drawing room, breathless.

"It's Madame Fournier," Lilah said. "She's gone."

"Gone?" James repeated.

"She took her luggage and left," Lilah explained. "And she must have gone on foot."

"She might have taken a cab," James pointed out.

"She can't have rung for one. I've been on the telephone with my agent since dinner," said Lilah. "And there's only the one line in the house."

"Ought we to go after her?" asked James.

"She was free to go whenever she pleased," Martha said. "We can't very well chase her down."

"Awful fishy, though."

"Everything about her was fishy," agreed Lilah.

"Indeed," said Camilla, her brow furrowed as if she were trying to do sums in her head.

Before James could decide whether to tell them that Madame

Fournier was Gladys Button, Marchand came to stand behind Lilah in the doorway.

"What's this about Madame Fournier having left?" he demanded

"Just that. She's gone," Lilah answered.

"Good God." Marchand's face was red and splotchy and he put a fist to his chest.

Lilah looked at her father, perplexed. "Whatever is the matter?"

"I—where are my pills?"

James got to his feet, operating on instinct alone. "Lie down on the sofa," he told the older man. "What pills? Digitalis?" he guessed. "Do you know where he keeps them, Lilah? All right, fetch them, will you? Martha, go get Carrow and have him bring the car around."

Lilah made for the door, but Camilla got to her feet instead, suddenly seeming to sober up. "You won't know where they are. I'll get them."

James arranged Marchand's hands over his head to improve blood flow. "Anthony, listen. What do you take the digitalis for?"

"My heart," the older man croaked, and then shut his eyes.

James sighed, and began to suspect that Marchand had prescribed these pills for himself without ever visiting a heart specialist or even a general practitioner. "Yes, but what *about* your heart? Heart failure? Arrhythmia?"

Marchand made a vague and useless sound of assent. His breaths were coming fast and his forehead was covered in sweat. With a sinking feeling, James realized this probably wasn't a simple attack of angina.

"Anthony," James said. "Stay awake." Marchand made no

response and James swore under his breath.

And then there was a firm hand on his shoulder. "Carrow's bringing the car round and I'll help you carry Marchand out," Leo said.

"Thank God. I worried you'd have already left." James felt the relief he always did in an emergency when there was somebody at hand who he could rely on. "His pulse is erratic," he said a moment later, examining his wristwatch. "Where in hell is Camilla? Lilah, find your mother and ask what's taking so long. Leo, go up to my bedroom and bring down my medical bag. You've seen it before, you know what it looks like. It's on top of the wardrobe."

There would be digitalis in James's bag; he carried it with him in case he was called to treat heart failure. But if Marchand's heart symptoms weren't due to his underlying heart condition and were instead—

He forced himself to think logically. Marchand's symptoms were typical of a heart attack. The only reason James was doubting this diagnosis was his knowledge that somebody in this house had secrets that might be worth killing over. That, and something he had seen out of the corner of his eye at dinner.

And the fact that Madame Fournier was gone.

And Camilla's missing Seconal.

Christ, he needed to think straight.

Leo returned, closing the door to the drawing room behind him. "Carrow just pulled up in front of the house. Do you want to give Marchand anything before we get him into the car?"

If Marchand had been poisoned or covertly administered a drug that interfered with his already dodgy heart, the best

175

James could do was administer activated charcoal. He couldn't administer both charcoal and digitalis, as the charcoal would likely prevent the digitalis from taking effect.

But it felt reckless to the point of madness to treat a man for poisoning when he was in the midst of what nearly all physicians would assume to be a heart attack. James was being paranoid. He was letting his own fears get the better of him.

James rummaged through his bag and removed the bottle of digitalis. Then he paused and took out the vial of activated charcoal. He swore and tossed the charcoal back into the bag.

"Hold his jaw open," James said, and Leo did so while James shoved a tablet into the back of Marchand's mouth and then dribbled in some water from a glass that Leo handed him. "Come on," James pleaded, then swore when Sir Anthony spit some of the water out.

James heard the door open. "His pill case was empty," said Lady Marchand.

Of bloody course it was. Well, it hardly mattered, as James had given him digitalis anyway, but who knew if the results would have been different if the man had got his medicine sooner. Marchand wasn't breathing at all now, blast him. "Have Carrow open the back door of the car, will you, Camilla?" That, at least, would get Camilla out of the room and prevent her from watching her husband go from bad to worse.

"Watch what I'm doing," James said to Leo, and pressed down on Marchand's chest a couple of times. "Now you do it." James bent forward and breathed into Marchand's mouth. The man's skin was getting cold, damn it all to hell, but James kept working, and Leo didn't say a word.

Finally, his forehead covered in sweat and his muscles aching, James paused to put his stethoscope to Marchand's heart.

CHAPTER TWENTY-FIVE

Nothing. He tossed it to the floor.

"Shit," Leo said.

James, still kneeling, buried his face in his hands. He had lost other patients—Christ, he had stopped counting during the war. And Sir Anthony wasn't even his patient, just a man who got sick when James happened to be his best bet for staying alive. But there was still the shock of it, the sense that he was supposed to have done better, the wrongness of being there when someone went from being a person to...not.

He felt a hand between his shoulder blades.

"Do you want me to tell Camilla and Lilah?" Leo asked.

James shook his head. "That's my job. But can you find Martha and let her know that the police will need to be called in, and then tell Carrow that we won't need the car after all? Christ."

"The police?" Leo echoed.

"A sudden death. A matter of routine."

"Maybe so, but that charcoal wasn't a matter of routine, was it?"

James recalled that Leo had enough experience with field medicine to know what activated charcoal was used for, and that it wasn't for treating heart attacks.

"The fact that I considered administering charcoal is why I can't avoid calling the police," James said.

"I'm so sorry," Leo started, but James cut him off.

"I can't think about it now. Damn it." And with that, James made for the door.

CHAPTER TWENTY-SIX

L eo remembered when James had sewed him up during the war. He had been just as he was that evening: efficient and calm, as if there was nothing he hadn't seen and nothing he wasn't equal to. Leo always got a satisfied little thrill when he remembered exactly what it was James did all day. It sounded so ordinary on the face of it: he was a country doctor with a slightly shabby surgery who spent his days treating chilblains and chest infections. He didn't have a practice on Harley Street; he would never be famous or celebrated for what he did. Leo knew enough of James's past to gather that his present career was a step down from what he had been aiming for before the war, when he had been a promising surgeon, when the realities of scalpel and sutures hadn't sent him into a blind panic. He was so quietly competent about what he did that sometimes it was easy to forget that he went about making people well, making lives better and sometimes outright saving them.

And now he was in the library with two policemen and Leo's heart hurt for him—not because he gave a damn about what happened to Marchand but because he cared about everything that happened to James.

The detectives hadn't left a uniformed officer outside the room to keep an eye on the house's occupants, from which Leo gathered that they were treating this as an accidental death and were simply talking to James as a physician who happened to be on the scene.

It also meant that Leo could position himself near the closed library door and overhear most of the conversation from within.

"As I said, I was worried he might have taken something that interacted badly with his digitalis, or perhaps that he had taken too much digitalis. It can happen, unfortunately, no matter how sternly doctors warn against taking more than we prescribe. Some people can't get over the idea that if one tablet is good, two will be better." James sounded weary.

"But Sir Anthony was a medical man himself, was he not?" asked the detective.

"We're notorious for making the worst patients. In any event, I suppose the postmortem will show if anything was amiss."

Leo heard the sounds of chairs being pushed back and men getting to their feet, and immediately backed away from the door.

After seeing the policemen out, James leaned against the closed door and shut his eyes. When he opened them, he noticed Leo sitting on the bench in the hall.

"You're still here," James said. There was a faint note of rebuke in his tone that Leo didn't know what to make of.

"Of course I am. Everyone has gone to bed," Leo said, his voice very quiet and gentle, "and Mr. Trevelyan went home."

James nodded again, not meeting Leo's eyes.

"You didn't expect me to go to the inn, did you?" Leo got to his feet and went to him. "I'm staying. It's late and I don't want to drive."

"I'm not going to have an episode or whatever it is you're worried about," James snapped. "I really only get that way with blood and gore, so you don't have to look after me."

"I know you don't," Leo said, hearing a soothing note in his voice that felt strange and out of place.

James visibly bristled. "I'm not as fragile as you think."

"I don't think you're fragile in the least, but if you want to argue, let's do it behind closed doors."

James headed upstairs, but once they were in the bedroom he retreated to the bathroom, and Leo soon heard the sound of the shower running.

When James emerged, a towel wrapped around his waist, Leo was laying James's pajamas out on the bed. He felt oddly caught out performing this act.

"You really don't have to do this," James said.

"Christ, James. I know I don't," Leo said, feeling defeated. "And I know I'm bad at this. I know you don't need me. You're past thirty and a goddamn doctor and you've been through hell all on your own. But I—fucking hell. Just take the goddamn pajamas, all right?"

James shot Leo a slightly startled look, but he put on the pajamas. He was doing up the last button before he spoke.

"Bad at what?" James asked. "You said you were bad at this."

Leo was crouched by the fireplace, attempting to start a fire using some coal that he had had pilfered from a small stockpile in the boiler room. "If I say 'looking after you,' are you going to take it as an insult? Because I don't mean it that way. I don't really know how to be a friend, let alone…" He made a vague gesture between them.

"That fire's never going to take."

"Ye of little faith," Leo muttered, and prodded a coal with a rolled-up piece of newspaper.

James sat beside him before the empty hearth. "You seem to be doing a fine job. Not at building the fire. At..." He made the same vague gesture between them, accompanied by a wry smile. "Not that I have all that much experience. But I don't have any complaints."

"That's because you have low standards and you let people walk all over you."

James looked like he wanted to argue, but instead he sighed. "No, it's because you're a lovely man."

Leo snorted. "Now I know you're full of it. Anyway, this is not the time to have this conversation. We're both tired and it's been a trying night."

"What conversation?"

Leo blamed weeks of exhaustion catching up with him. "The one where I point out that your worst fear—the one about people putting knives and bullets and poisons into one another? That's me. That's my life's work."

"No it isn't."

Leo jabbed the poker into the smoldering coals. "I know what my job is, James."

"I mean it isn't my worst fear. It's a hang-up. It's faulty wiring." He passed a hand over his jaw. "What I'm worried about—the thing that keeps me up at night—is war. My brain apparently isn't sophisticated enough to develop a phobia of war, so instead I'm fixated on gore and blood."

"Oh."

"I *have* been to a psychologist, you know. It didn't work out with Marchand, but I did see someone else for a while. Also, I don't know the exact details of your job, but we both know plenty of people whose job actually was to put bullets and knives and whatnot into people. That's literally what soldiers do, Leo. And I'm not afraid of them as individuals."

Leo understood all this. James's words made sense and ought to be reassuring, but instead they made all the inchoate doubts that had been swirling around his mind for the past few weeks coalesce into something he couldn't avoid. "I can't keep doing it."

James went rigid. "Can't keep..." He made that same gesture, back and forth between them.

"What? Lord, no, not that. I can't keep on doing my job."

James nodded slowly and took Leo's hand, then brushed his lips over the knuckles. "All right."

"All right? That's it? You're not going to tell me to stop?"

"It's not my place."

Leo wanted to scream. He wanted James to see that it *was* his place, but he also didn't want James to say a bloody thing about it because if James spoke, it would be offers and promises and Leo couldn't handle that. He moved out of his crouching position so he was sitting beside James, his arms wrapped around his knees.

"I can't wait to see what you do next," James said.

For the first time in his adult life, Leo felt in danger of crying, so instead he cleared his throat and looked away and did useless things to the fire.

But James evidently had had enough. He gently took hold of Leo's hands, then straddled his lap. "Thank you for the pajamas."

"I'm sorry that old arsehole died on you," Leo mumbled into James's collar. "Actually, I just wish he'd waited to die until after he got back to London."

CHAPTER TWENTY-SIX

"Do you want me to tell you why I was worried about poison?" James asked.

"Are you sure you want to?" Leo asked, pulling back just enough to see James's face.

"Earlier in the day, Camilla said her medicine was missing. She takes Seconal, a barbiturate."

"Would a barbiturate overdose cause a heart attack?"

"With a barbiturate overdose, one worries about the heart slowing to the point that it stops entirely, which is not at all what happened tonight. But there was something odd that happened during dinner."

"Madame's spilled wine glass?" Leo asked.

"Exactly. Plenty of opportunity to slip something into Marchand's glass during the confusion."

"But who would want to poison him? Assuming Madame is Gladys Button—and I still see no reason not to—and she was blackmailing him, she had every reason to wish to keep him alive."

"Who else might have had the opportunity? Mrs. Carrow could have put something in his glass while she was setting the table," James said. "But I can't think what motive she'd have, or how she could be sure where Sir Anthony would sit. There were no place cards and no attempt to sort out precedence. No, it had to have happened during the spill. The glasses could have been switched, I suppose. Marchand might have put something in Madame's glass, maybe hoping to get rid of his blackmailer, and then Madame either accidentally or deliberately switched the glasses."

James stared at him. "I *love* that your mind works that way."

Leo blinked. "What."

"You think it puts me off, but you're wrong."

Leo was pretty sure the strange heat in his face was a blush; this was truly a night of horrific firsts. "We don't even know if he was poisoned.

"Did you notice whether the police took the glasses from the dining room table?"

"Yes, and they took samples of food with them as well, although that stew was in a single dish and we all ladled out our own portions, so I suspect that's out."

"So we ought to know in a few days?"

"Give or take." Leo drummed his fingers on his knee. "Let's go to bed and think about this in the morning." He let himself be pulled to his feet and into James's waiting embrace.

CHAPTER TWENTY-SEVEN

The first rays of sunlight were streaming through the window when Leo woke. That meant it was probably around seven o'clock, and since they hadn't managed to get to sleep until past two, Leo could have done with quite a bit more sleep. But there were things to do—he didn't care how many murders took place at Blackthorn, he still wanted to get James back to Wychcomb St. Mary that night, which meant he needed to get to work as soon as possible. Gingerly, so as not to disturb James, he tried to slide out from under James's arm. But he must not have moved carefully enough, because James opened the eye that wasn't pressed into his pillow.

"Too early," James mumbled. "Back to bed."

"Sleep. I'll be back in an hour with tea."

"I'll come with you," James said, sitting up.

"No, no. You can sleep for another hour, so you might as well."

It spoke to how tired James must have been that he lay back down without a protest and was fast asleep by the time Leo was dressed.

When Leo reached the stairs, instead of going down, he continued straight, toward a group of rooms that were on the opposite side of the house from the guest rooms. Here, he hoped to find Martha Dauntsey's bedroom and maybe the late Mr. Bellamy's.

He passed what had to be Martha Dauntsey's room, door ajar and bed hastily made. In the corner was a bookshelf jammed full of volumes, the accumulated reading of a lifetime, if Leo judged correctly. By the window stood a writing desk, and next to it an armchair with threadbare upholstery. Everything in the room was worn and tired-looking, shabby in the way that well-loved homes often were.

Across the hall was another room that might once have been a family bedroom but was now a box room. The walls were papered with a floral pattern that might once have been red, but which had long since faded to a tepid blush. Leo wondered if this might have been Rose's room. On a whim, he stepped to the window and threw it open. When he stuck his head out, he could see a sliver of gray winter sea. It was his first glimpse of the sea since he had arrived here. He could also plainly see the door of the lodge. Carrow was already awake, smoking a cigarette.

Further down the corridor was a room that could only be Rupert Bellamy's. It had the same well-worn comfort of Miss Dauntsey's bedroom, only more opulent. He turned in place, taking in the photographs on the wall. They were much like any other collection of family photographs, except that the people in these were richer than most. Especially in the older pictures, the women were all but draped in pearls and jewels. He caught sight of an honest-to-god tiara in one photograph.

There was Lady Marchand at about twelve years old, looking like she was on her way to church—white gloves, clean pinafore, neatly curled hair—and beside her was a girl who looked like she had been dragged head-first out of a tree and shoved into a frock against her will.

Another photograph showed a man and a girl with dark hair and similar profiles, about fifty and twenty respectively. They wore riding clothes and stood beside an enormous black horse they both seemed inordinately proud of. Leo didn't give a fig about that horse, or any horse for that matter. Instead, he looked at the woman who had disappeared and caused all this trouble. He looked at her face, as if something there might tell him her secrets.

There wasn't anything, of course. She was just an ordinary rich girl.

A few frames over was a picture of what appeared to be Lady Marchand's wedding day. So, this was the party that had taken James away from his cricket match. Camilla wore a gown that Leo could tell, even at a remove of twenty years, must have cost a small fortune and weighed at least a stone. Sir Anthony, Leo was irked to admit, was almost devastatingly handsome in the usual cutaway and tails.

Rose was in the picture as well, looking vaguely uncomfortable in a way that Leo couldn't pinpoint. She had been much happier in the picture with the horse. So had her father, come to that. Well, it stood to reason—other than the newlyweds, people rarely looked happy in wedding photographs.

Off to the side in the wedding photograph stood a grim-faced boy in cutaways. Leo almost laughed, because he had seen that same expression on James's face too many times. It was one of his favorite expressions, though he'd never tell James—that look of dutiful resignation with which he answered calls from patients at horrible hours, or when he did some other unpleasant task that he was too honorable to even dream of shirking. That's what James was, an honorable man; Leo had always scoffed at honor as a means for men to let themselves become emotionally overwrought over trifles, but in James it was something else. It was something solid and reliable and good.

Leo scanned the photos and sighed. They did nothing but illustrate the parts of a story that he already understood. There was another, apparently separate story that was hidden from these photographs, but which Leo could see just as clearly: a pickpocket-turned-maid who ran away, a man who married an heiress but had no money, and a woman who disappeared.

Satisfied that he had seen all he needed to see, Leo moved quietly down the stairs, more from instinct than from any real fear of being discovered.

The police had locked the dining room and the door was still shut. He debated picking the lock and seeing for himself whether there were any traces of powder in the wine glasses, but doubted that the police would have left that kind of evidence sitting around.

Leo really ought to have checked the wine glasses himself last night, between the time Marchand died and the arrival of the police. But at the time he had been more concerned with James. The police, after all, could be relied on to put liquids in little vials and test for common substances. There was nothing to be lost by letting them do their job—no national secrets would be compromised and James wouldn't be put in danger.

The realization that his list of priorities began and ended with national secrets and James Sommers, and probably not even in that order, didn't come as a surprise.

The kitchen was empty but the kettle was warm. Martha,

he supposed, must have made herself some tea already. He put the kettle back on the hob and set about making himself a cup; he'd wait to make James's until a bit later so it didn't get cold. He didn't bother scrounging for sugar or milk and instead took his cup of black tea outside.

It was cold but not frigid as he made his way along the perimeter of the house. The sun was now high enough in the sky for him to get a good look at Blackthorn. It was, he supposed, not actively hideous, if one went in for twee faux-gothic nooks and crannies and pretty little embellishments.

Leo did not go in for any of those things. If pressed to choose a style of architecture he did go in for, he'd choose something spare and modern without any of these embarrassing excesses.

But then he'd remember James's house—their house? James thought so, but he was not a reliable source of information on this topic—and its quaint window seat and pointless little gable. And he'd have to concede that his definition of what a home ought to look like was out of alignment with all his aesthetic principles.

Blackthorn, in any event, could be dismissed as a failure both aesthetically and also according to whatever muddled feelings Leo was inclined to apply to James-related things.

"It's not that bad," said a voice.

Leo turned to see Camilla, a cup of tea cradled in her hands. She was standing in the middle of a patch of dead grass, looking at a tree that was just beginning to come into leaf. She wore a coat over what appeared to be a dressing gown, and her dark hair was loose around her shoulders. Without makeup or her hair dressed, she looked remarkably like the photograph he had seen of Rupert Bellamy. Something about the set of her jaw and the way her hands clasped her teacup made him decide not to offer condolences on the loss of her husband.

"It's not my idea of a seaside home," Leo said instead. "You wouldn't even know you were near the ocean, let alone within a stone's throw of the shore." Leo's knowledge of seaside holidays was entirely theoretical but conjured images of either Brighton or Monte Carlo and not many places in between.

"Nor is it mine. It is where I grew up, though. Where are you from, Mr. Page?"

Yesterday he would have assumed that this line of questioning was meant to determine his pedigree, but there was something almost candid in the way she asked now. "Bristol," he said, which was at least the partial truth. "But it's been years since I've been back."

"Sometimes it's better that way." Camilla took a sip of her tea.

At some point in the past twenty-four hours, her accent had unraveled and so had her posture. What had been an almost mincing RP was now looser; the way she sat could almost be described as slouching. He'd have chalked these changes up to the loss of her husband, but he had noticed them yesterday at dinner as well. He saw in Camilla the signs of someone who had spent so long—years, maybe decades—checking her impulses, but something had happened yesterday to make her drain a bottle of wine and throw caution to the wind.

Leo knew what it was like to finally stop checking impulses, to finally acknowledge that there was someone inside who *had* impulses. He had let the contours of his world be shaped entirely by his work, and Camilla had perhaps done something similar—but instead of work, she served some other god. Her husband? Propriety? He didn't know, and it probably didn't matter. What mattered was that something had happened to make Camilla cast off the things she had once thought paramount.

Leo thought of that Gainsborough landscape that hung on the dining room wall, the one that had been left to Camilla in her father's will. It was almost grotesque in its departure from reality, with its cheerful peasants and fat cows, its serene ocean and pillowy boulders. Maybe he was making too much of it, but this whole family was so dedicated to looking away from anything difficult that he wondered if they really saw the world through a gauzy screen. What must it be like for that screen to be whipped away? Is that what had happened to Camilla?

"I was beastly to James," Camilla said.

"I doubt that very much." As far as Leo could tell, she and James had hardly spoken.

"I didn't keep in touch with him after Rose—after everything. Anthony said it would be kinder to let James forget about what happened here, to let him get on with things. But I shouldn't have listened to him."

Leo looked at Camilla, really looked at her, and listened to what she was saying. Her husband had died not twelve hours earlier and she was thinking of his past misdeed—and how she had been complicit.

"He's too kind to hold a grudge about such a thing even if he ought to," Camilla went on.

"Daresay you're right." Leo, on the other hand, would happily carry all James's grudges for him.

"I know I am. People do change from who they are as children, but they don't change fundamentally."

When his offer to fetch another blanket was waved away, Leo left Lady Marchand in the garden. He returned to the kitchen, where he brewed another cup of tea—this time ransacking the cupboards until he found the sugar bowl—and brought it up to James.

When Leo opened the bedroom door, James rolled over to face him, his face lit up with a sleepy surprise. Leo sat on the edge of the bed and handed him the cup. "What do I need to do," Leo asked, "for you to expect to see me walk through doors?"

"It's not that I expect you to run off," James said. He leaned against the pillows, his hair pushed around in all directions the way it always was in the morning, all cowlicks and disorder.

Leo could, and probably should, leave it there. The alternative was a conversation about—he didn't quite know what it would be about. His feelings? His devotion? Both sounded terrible. But if the alternative was James not believing that Leo would stick around, then he'd muddle through it. "You just don't expect me to come back."

"Not that either." James idly brushed his knuckles against Leo's knee. "It seems so implausible that I get to have you around. Not because of who you are or what you do, but because it's lovely and I suppose I'm not in the habit of expecting lovely things."

"You should be," Leo said, too fast and too urgent. This was all wrong. It ought to be *Leo* who felt like he didn't deserve good things. James deserved everything good in the world, and how could he be so stupid as not to realize this?

"Sweetheart," James said, and Leo felt his cheeks heat. "Perhaps I'm just not used to *keeping* lovely things."

"Get used to it," Leo grumbled, and then couldn't take much more of that so he got to his feet and busied himself in packing their bags and in general tidying up. "Whose jacket is this?"

he asked, holding up an unfamiliar garment. "Harris tweed, too large to be either of ours." He knew the answer even as he asked the question.

"That was Marchand's. I took his coat off in order to do chest compressions, and I took my own coat off at the same time. They must have got mixed up and Martha brought it here by mistake."

Out of habit or professional instinct or just plain nosiness, Leo began turning out the pockets. A few shillings, a button, a length of string, a folded-up piece of paper—exactly what you'd find in anyone's pocket. He unfolded the paper. But instead of a scrawled telephone number or shopping list, it was a note: "I saw what you did by the cherry tree. A thousand pounds by ten p.m."

CHAPTER TWENTY-EIGHT

However much sleep he had managed the previous night had been a drop in the ocean, and James struggled to clear the fog of exhaustion from his thoughts. "That's what Gladys meant in the phone call you overheard, right? She said she had given him until that night—she must have been referring to giving Marchand that note."

"That's what it looks like." Leo tossed a clean shirt and a pair of trousers on the bed for James to change into. "But then why in hell did she run off before collecting her money?"

"Unless she didn't run off." James dragged himself out of bed and stripped off his pajamas, shivering in the cold air before hastily dressing.

"Nobody in this house or the lodge had time to kill anyone and dispose of their body. Between dinner and the time Gladys was missed, I was with the Carrows and you were with Camilla and Martha."

"And Sir Anthony was shocked to discover that Gladys was gone. I don't think he could have been faking it."

"Who noticed Gladys was gone?"

"Lilah. And she has an alibi too—she was on the telephone.

194

That can be checked up on." James was surprised that he didn't even balk at this idea, but at the moment all he cared about was getting to the bottom of this mess and then getting home.

Leo frowned. "Why would Lilah have gone to look for Gladys? She didn't even know that Madame Fournier was Gladys, did she?"

"I can't see how she would."

"Hmm. That tree between the house and the lodge," Leo said, grabbing a few stray items from various surfaces and dropping them pell-mell into James's valise. "Is it a cherry tree?"

"Yes," said James. "But it's new. It wasn't there in 1927. Back then, a couple of fruit trees were in the front garden."

"It can't be that new. It's quite large. I just ran into Lady Marchand by that tree."

"What on earth was Camilla doing out of doors at this hour?"

"Drinking tea and staring at cherry trees, evidently."

James shot an alarmed look at Leo. "We need to talk to Camilla and Martha."

"I'm afraid we do."

First, though, they went downstairs to use the telephone. James rang the Three Bells in the village to ask if anyone answering Gladys Button's description had taken a room there, and when that proved a dead end, Leo rang the grocer's wife.

"Of course Gladys isn't here. Where'd you get an idea like that?" James heard Mrs. Mudge say, her voice loud enough that he could hear it while standing on the threshold of the telephone room.

By now, they had attracted the attention of Martha and Lilah, who hovered behind them in the hall. Succinctly, James explained that two menacing notes had been found, but left out that one had been found in Sir Anthony's bedroom and the other in his pocket. The man had been Lilah's father, after all, and he had died not twelve hours earlier. She could be spared the knowledge that he was apparently being blackmailed, possibly for some secret related to Rose's disappearance.

"The cherry tree?" Martha repeated. "What can that have to do with anything?"

"When was it planted?" James asked, a realization dawning on him.

Martha stared at him, her face going gray. "It was planted during the summer of 1927 while I was away," she said, not looking at Lilah. "I remember because it was planted in the most foolish place, quite the wrong spot for a cherry tree, and by the time I returned, it was too late to transplant. It seemed such a silly thing to fret over, considering all the other things there were to be upset about, but I was cross all the same."

James looked at the three people around him. Martha, worried and shaken. Lilah, unnaturally serious. Leo, looking as if this were all desperately familiar. He wondered who would finally say aloud what they all must be thinking.

In the end, he spoke up himself. "We have to dig it up."

Martha drew in a sharp breath. Lilah gave a single nod. Leo stepped closer to him.

The thought of what might be buried beneath that tree made James's vision darken at the edges. Something worth blackmail; a secret worth a thousand pounds. Something worth twenty years of secrecy. The idea made his stomach turn. But he knew that he had to dig it up himself. Martha could hardly do it, and Lilah had on silk stockings, and they certainly couldn't pester Carrow to do some impromptu gravedigging, or grave robbing, or whatever they were—

"I saw where Carrow keeps the shovels," said Leo, already

striding toward the door. "I'll handle it."

James followed him into the gray winter day. "You don't need—"

"Bollocks on need. One of us is fine with this sort of thing and the other isn't and that's that."

James strongly doubted that Leo, or anyone, was *fine* with the prospect of possibly digging up a body, or a skeleton, or whatever they were afraid of finding. But he probably wouldn't faint or break down while doing it, so that put him one up on James. And there was something about the way he had looked at James while speaking, as if daring James to stop him from doing this for him.

"Thank you," he said, holding Leo's gaze. Leo gave him a quick nod.

Camilla was at the tree again. She wore a tweed skirt and coat and the wind whipped through her hair.

"What's going on?" she asked as Leo stepped on the shovel and broke ground.

"Why were you out here this morning?" James asked.

"Because Rose asked for it to be planted. The old tree had stopped producing fruit and she knew how Martha and I were about cherry preserves." Her eyes were wide and clear, and James would have sworn she was telling the truth. "And I miss her."

"That's all?"

"What else would it be?" But even as she asked the question, her gaze was locked on Leo and the shovel. "What's happening?" she asked.

James didn't answer.

"This doesn't make sense." She gripped James's arm. "You've got this all wrong. You expect to find Rose, but that can't be

197

right."

"Why don't you go inside," James suggested gently. "You've had a hell of a twenty-four hours." *And it's not going to get any easier*, he didn't say.

"You can't seriously expect me to go lie down while you're out here attempting to dig up my sister's body," Camilla said. Her words cut through the sound of the wind and the steady slice of Leo's shovel cutting through the dirt. James was faintly shocked that it was Camilla, of all people, who gave voice to the thing that so far none of them had spoken aloud.

"No, I suppose not," James conceded.

"Why not just tell me what's going on?"

"We found a note that said 'I saw what you did by the cherry tree' in your husband's pocket. There's reason to believe he was being blackmailed."

The hole was knee deep now. James was struck by the sudden thought, both ghastly and somehow reassuring, that this was not the first time Leo had been called upon to dig a hole six feet deep.

The clouds, which had been threatening rain since that morning, finally broke. James looked at Camilla, at the raindrops landing on her face. That day when she had brought him tea and biscuits in his bedroom, she had been crying, he remembered. What had happened to make her go from tears at her sister's disappearance to calmly saying it was none of her business? Was her change in attitude because she was covering up for her husband? Except—James found it hard to believe that she could remain married to a man she knew to have killed her sister.

"You think Anthony killed Rose," Camilla said finally, leveling him with a challenging stare that reminded him of nobody so much as Rose herself, and maybe a little of Lilah.

"I don't know," he answered. "But something happened here."

Lilah came up to them. "Should we call the police?"

"And tell them what?" James asked. "We can wait until we…" He didn't dare finish that sentence. What had been in the family for so long could stay there for another hour or so.

Leo paused to wipe rain off his forehead, and James cursed himself for not having packed his Macintosh. Leo, at least, had his overcoat. It seemed that Leo had struck a root. He moved a few feet to the side to begin another hole. James went to him and put his hand over Leo's on the shovel handle. "I'll spell you."

"Let me do this," said Leo, a little out of breath, his hair damp with rain. In his words James heard an unspoken *for you* that he couldn't, wouldn't reject. He just nodded his head and went back to Camilla. Lilah stood by Martha, holding her arm as if preventing her from moving closer.

And toward the back of their morbid gathering, sheltered by the eaves of the lodge, stood Carrow, his cap pulled low over his forehead and his hands in his pocket.

Over the sound of the rain was a dull thud as the metal shovel struck something. James could see Lilah's brow furrow in a confusion mirroring his own; whatever horrors were in that hole shouldn't clank against a shovel.

Leo, now standing in the hole, crouched so low that James could only see the top of his head. "I need a spade," he called, and it was Carrow who came forward with one.

There came more sounds of metal against metal and then, finally, Leo lifted a box of some sort out of the hole and placed it on the ground. With a hand from Carrow, Leo hoisted himself out of the hole and crouched down to examine the box.

"What is it?" Lilah asked. But James wasn't paying attention to her. His attention was divided between Leo, who was attempting to pry the box open with a pocketknife, and Camilla, whose body was suddenly devoid of tension. Whatever was happening, this made sense to her.

James knelt on the ground beside Leo. The object appeared to be a metal toolbox, now blackened with age and dirt and covered in rust. The hinges weren't budging and neither was the latch.

"We'll have to break it," Leo muttered. Then he did something with his knife that made the hinges give way. The box sprang open.

It was empty.

Behind them, Carrow burst into laughter.

CHAPTER TWENTY-NINE

L eo, soaked to the bone, sat in the kitchen, the empty metal box open before him on the table.

"Why would anyone bury an empty box?" he asked. But of course nobody buried empty boxes. Somebody had buried this box when it had something in it, and then someone else had stolen its contents. *That* was what Gladys had seen.

"I suppose my father took whatever was in it?" asked Lilah.

"I had hoped you hadn't overheard any of that," said James.

"There was no love lost between my father and myself," Lilah said. "And I think you know it. He always did his best to make me feel weak and troublesome, as if I were a disaster waiting to happen."

Her words crystalized something in Leo's thoughts. "He told Rose she needed a doctor." He caught James's eye. At first, they had thought that perhaps Marchand was advising a troubled and possibly suicidal Rose to see a psychiatrist. Then they had wondered whether he meant she needed to see a doctor to advise her about her pregnancy. But she hadn't been suicidal, and she hadn't been pregnant. "Why might that have been?" he asked carefully, because Lilah didn't know there was any mystery surrounding who may or may not have been pregnant that summer.

"He was always telling people they needed doctors," Lilah said. "He did it to you yesterday in the drawing room, James."

James drew in a breath. "Damn it, he did." He turned to Leo. "He said a lot of nonsense about how I needed to stop practicing medicine and get to an asylum or risk a complete breakdown."

"He was a bully, but he tricked people into thinking he was concerned and that he knew their minds better than they did," Lilah said.

"What if he did that to Rose?" Leo asked. "What if she told him something sensitive? Or, more likely, what if he found out." He kept his gaze fixed on the box as he spoke, knowing that James would understand that they were talking about Rose preferring women, and not wanting to give away too much of their own secrets in front of Lilah.

"And then he told she was unwell," James said darkly.

"We're talking about Aunt Rose being a lesbian, yes?" Lilah asked, sounding tired. "You know, I was at dinner yesterday too. I've spent twenty years learning to decipher Bellamy subtext."

"Yes, well," James said, sounding sheepish. "Would your father have assumed a lesbian needed psychological treatment?"

"What do you think, James," Lilah sighed. "Of course he would have. And he *has*."

"He told her she needed a doctor," Leo repeated, only half paying attention to James and Lilah's conversation. What else might he have said? Was he threatening her or goading her? Was he telling her what would happen if she stayed or trying to make her leave—or trying to insinuate that she ought to do worse?

Leo got to his feet so abruptly the chair started to tip over before James caught it. "I've been *blind*. Lilah, I need you to speak to your mother." And then he told Lilah what he needed to know.

Leo thought about what he knew. A series of photographs. A person who knew they were queer, and all the ways a conservative family and a conventional doctor could punish them for that. All the good reasons for which a person might leave everything behind.

Leo knew about secrets. Professionally his life revolved around secrets, but privately it did as well. What he and James were to one another was, and had to be, a secret. There were secrets that destroyed, but there were also secrets that created.

"What time is it?" Leo asked.

"It's only ten," James answered.

That gave them two hours before Mr. Trevelyan returned and expected an answer to the question Rupert Bellamy had posed in his will. "I have to speak to Carrow. Will you come?"

James was already on his feet. Before leaving the kitchen, he braced an arm against the closed door and drew Leo to him with a hand at the small of his back. "Do you want to tell me what's going on?"

"Not yet," Leo said, taking a moment to rest his forehead against the solid warmth of James's shoulder. "I ought to speak to Carrow first."

"All right," James said slowly and without protest, smoothing a hand up Leo's back. "Is Carrow somehow mixed up in this? Don't tell me he's the chauffeur."

Leo let out a short laugh. "I can tell you that I haven't the faintest idea where that chauffeur went or what became of him." That was about the only thread of the tangle he hadn't worked loose, and he hoped Carrow could help him with that as well. Reluctantly, he pulled away.

Leo pushed open the back door and passed through, James following him. It had stopped raining, but it was cold and wet, without a patch of blue in the sky or fleck of green on the ground.

Mrs. Carrow opened the door to them right away.

"I'm sorry to trouble you," Leo said as she ushered them in. "Is Carrow here?"

"Been wondering when you'd show up," Carrow said from the kitchen. He stood before a tray of cooling biscuits that bore a conspicuously empty spot. He had a crumb at the corner of his mouth. Leo fervently hoped he wasn't going to disturb the peace of this couple.

"I'll be quick," Leo said. "But before I start, I want you to know that I can keep secrets, and so can James." As he watched, Carrow swallowed and looked at something over Leo's shoulder—his wife, Leo guessed. "How much was in that box? Was it the full twenty thousand?"

Something that was almost a smile crossed Carrow's face. "God, no. Ten. I took five with me and paid the other five to John Davis—the chauffeur—for helping me."

Miriam Carrow *tsk*ed. "Daft thing to do, burying money like that, I always said."

"And you were right, love. In my defense, I was twenty-one. It seemed a grand idea at the time. I wanted to know that I could come back to it, if I ever got desperate."

Leo supposed that it counted for something that he hadn't been desperate, that for twenty years he hadn't seen the need to try to dig up his inheritance. "Is that why you insisted the tree be planted? You knew you were going to run away, and you wanted a convenient hiding place for the money and a way to mark it?"

Carrow nodded. "I suppose Gladys saw me and couldn't resist. Can't blame her."

Leo and James exchanged a glance. "We don't think it was Gladys."

"Who, then? Oh, bugger me. Marchand? He always was a shifty bastard. How did you know?" Carrow asked. "About me, I mean."

"It's just that you look remarkably like your father," Leo said carefully, "once one knows what to look for. There was a photograph of you both standing next to a horse, both wearing almost identical riding kit. Can Martha and Camilla really not know?"

Carrow sank into a chair and gestured for Leo and James to join him. "People don't see what they don't want to see. Or what they aren't expecting to see, I suppose. There were times I thought my father knew. How did you really guess? It can't just have been the resemblance."

"No, it wasn't, and it took me until this morning, I'm ashamed to admit. The people who knew you best were quite certain you'd never take up with a man, but at the same time there were rumors flying about the village about you coming and going from the chauffeur's quarters." The chauffeur's quarters, which were, Leo remembered, this very building. "There was gossip about you leaving your clothes behind. And your family talked about how you preferred to go about in trousers and crop your hair short. That all might add up to nothing, but it could also mean that the chauffeur was your ally, that he set you up with clothes and a place to get changed and then drove you off to wherever you lived the way you wanted to live."

"Mostly I just sat around here," Carrow said. Mrs. Carrow had come to stand beside him, a hand clamped over his shoulder. Carrow rested his own hand over hers.

"But Anthony Marchand found out."

"He wanted to have me sent to an institution. For my own good, of course, and to spare Camilla the shame of having a deviant sister."

"And so, instead of risking losing your freedom, you left," Leo said.

"Yes, but also I had to get out if I wanted to be free. I couldn't be Rose Bellamy. I couldn't be the person they thought I was, and I couldn't explain to them what it was I needed. I wanted to start fresh, and so I did." He said these last words simply but not, Leo thought, without pride.

"I suppose that all I need to know is whether you want James and me to keep our mouths shut or whether you plan to come forward to inherit the estate."

Carrow and Mrs. Carrow exchanged a look. "We've already talked about this," said Carrow. "I don't want the Bellamy estate. When I left, I made the choice to leave all that behind, and I meant it. I still mean it. What I have now, I earned. My life, my living, and my name are mine, and I don't want to undo that." He turned his attention to James. "You've turned out every bit as well as I knew you would, Jamie."

There was nothing to risk, not in this company, so Leo reached out and squeezed James's thigh under the table, and then didn't let go. "Do you mean to tell Martha and Camilla?"

"No," said Carrow. "I prefer my life the way it is. I have friends and I have Miriam. I don't want to expose myself to hatred and rejection. I don't owe that to any of them. Martha's quite fond of me, as she's come to know me. And so was my father. As for Camilla..." His cheeks flushed. "I send her a Christmas letter every year."

"Camilla knew all this time that you were alive and didn't say anything? I wouldn't have thought she had it in her."

"I don't think she recognized me. She really needs spectacles but is too vain to wear them. But even if she had been able to see me properly, I don't think she would have recognized me—not like this, and not after twenty years. All I told her in the letters was that I was alive and well, and that I wished her the best."

"She's said several times that your reasons for leaving were none of our business and that we ought to leave well enough alone," James said.

"One could always rely on Camilla not to think too terribly hard about anything," he said, smiling faintly. "But, my God, she's loyal, never to breathe a word of it."

"Madame—I mean Gladys Button. She recognized you, didn't she. I saw her speaking with you," James said.

"Yes," said Carrow.

"She didn't make trouble for you, did she?"

"No, she had spent twenty years thinking I was dead and that my brother-in-law had killed me. She only wanted to know whether he was dangerous."

"And what did you tell her?" Leo asked.

"That I didn't know," said Carrow. "And that a lot depends on your definition of dangerous."

And that, Leo realized, might partly explain why Gladys had run, but he'd think more about that later.

"If I can just ask you one more question." Leo looked at Carrow. "Why did you come back to Blackthorn?"

"My father wasn't well," Carrow said. "We had been close, back when I was young. I wanted to look after him. Even though I didn't know if he was capable of knowing me as his child, I hoped that he could know me as someone who cared for him. Miriam was good enough to go along with it."

"It's a good house," Mrs. Carrow said, gesturing around her. "Not bad for no rent and only a little cooking. I do a fair trade with my landscapes in the summer. And we've almost got enough saved to buy the garage in town, now, if we want to stay."

And maybe it was as simple as that—you made compromises for the people you loved. Sometimes they were gifts bestowed on the undeserving—looking after a father who might have cast you out if he knew the truth of who you were. Sometimes they were small—cooking an extra meal and washing some dishes in order to smooth things over for the man you loved.

Maybe that was what it took to build a life—the recognition that there was always going to be someone giving and someone taking. It didn't have to be equal and it didn't have to even make sense. It could be completely irrational and even misguided, and really that was the best hope Leo had, enough to make him feel downright optimistic as he and James stepped back outside into the chilly February day.

CHAPTER THIRTY

"Let's walk to the sea," James said when they left the lodge. "We still have a little time before Mr. Trevelyan is due to arrive." He glanced at Leo, whose hands were deep in his pockets and whose shoulders were hunched.

It was an ugly day, gray and damp and dreary. It was the sort of day best spent near a fire, and James couldn't say what possessed him to want to see the ocean except that it felt like a waste to be a stone's throw from the sea and not bother to take so much as a look at it.

They had walked for a few minutes when their silence began to strike James as strained. He nudged Leo with his elbow. "Out with it."

Leo sighed, and it sounded like capitulation. "I keep expecting you to come to your senses."

This wasn't the first time Leo had said this sort of thing, and previously James had—well, not exactly dismissed it, but told Leo he had nothing to worry about. But now that seemed wrong. It seemed like something that the Bellamys would do: find something unpleasant or difficult and refuse to look at it.

So he swallowed hard. "I feel pretty much the same way,

actually."

"Really?"

"I suppose it'll wear off after a while. And we have a while. We have all the time we want."

They walked the rest of the short distance to the sea, and it was just as dark and unpleasant as James could have predicted, but he felt better seeing it anyway, and even better because Leo was at his side, plainly humoring him, valiantly attempting to light a cigarette in the wind.

"Yesterday you said something about how I had invited my worst nightmare into my life," James said.

"I was being maudlin and all I did was embarrass myself," Leo griped. "Don't remind me."

"No, listen. I'm not inviting you into my life," James said. "I'm trying to live my life with you." That wasn't quite right either. "I want us to live our lives together. Or *a* life."

"Still think you're mad."

"Could be. But if you were—if I were—Christ almighty, if it were possible, I'd have had you at the registrar's office weeks ago."

James could almost *hear* Leo's blush. "Nobody would marry you in a registrar's office," Leo finally said, sounding strangled. "It'd be a church or nothing."

And that—that was Leo not arguing with the premise. That was Leo *accepting* the premise. "You're probably right," James agreed.

"People would say we were being hasty," Leo said.

"Pfft. Half the married couples I know got hitched within weeks of meeting. War, you know. We'd be boring." James's heart felt like it was in danger of beating out of his chest.

"That's me, boring."

They were alone on the beach, the tide halfway out, and the wind fiercer than it had been back at Blackthorn. Leo deliberately turned up James's collar and adjusted his muffler.

They returned to the house in a silence that felt settled and satisfied, their shoulders bumping and the backs of their hands brushing together.

Camilla stood in front of Blackthorn, a shawl wrapped around her shoulders. She looked ten years older than she had two days earlier. Her hair was still down and her dark clothes were silhouetted against the gray stone of the house. She looked like nothing so much as a woman on the cover of a penny dreadful.

And she was apparently waiting for them, or at least for James.

"Lilah said that you wanted to know whether Anthony needed money in the summer of 1927," she said bluntly. "He needed capital to buy a colleague's practice, and I wasn't due to get my inheritance until the following year."

"And did he get the money?"

She smiled tightly. "He said he was able to arrange something. I never asked questions about money."

James remembered the look Camilla and Lilah had shared the previous afternoon in the library when James had revealed that Rose's bank account was empty. Camilla had known then, James was sure of it. She probably didn't know how her husband had got his hands on her sister's money—on *Carrow's* money—but she knew he had something to do with it.

"He didn't want her to come back," Camilla said. "If she came back, she might discover that the money was missing. All those things he told the police, all of it was intended to make it look like she was dead. How was she meant to come

211

back after that?"

James knew that the truth was more complicated: Carrow had other reasons not to come back, but the knowledge that his brother-in-law might institutionalize him had to be at the top of the list. So while Camilla might have the details wrong, she was right in the sense that her husband had been complicit in her sibling's disappearance.

"Anthony killed her, in a way," Camilla said. "It was a kind of killing."

Before James could wonder why she had phrased it this way, Mr. Trevelyan's car rolled into the drive and it was time to go inside.

As the guests gathered in the library to meet one last time, the mood in the room was even more fraught with anticipation than it had been two days earlier.

Lilah sat at one end of the sofa, one leg crossed over the other while she read a fashion magazine. Camilla sat beside her, gazing off into the distance fretfully. Martha perched on the edge of the armchair by the fire, her fists clenched on the arms of the chair. James sat in the chair opposite her, Leo at his side, his back to the fire.

Once again, the Carrows stood in the doorway.

Mr. Trevelyan cleared his throat. At that moment, the casement clock in the hall struck twelve. While it chimed out the hour, everyone shifted uncomfortably, the way one always does when an overly loud clock makes its presence known.

"I suppose the estate will pass to the home for wayward girls or whatever charity struck Father's fancy," Camilla said, for all the world as if she was supremely uninterested in the fate of Blackthorn or her father's money.

"Not exactly," said Mr. Trevelyan. "I did receive a solution."

Everyone sat up a little straighter, suddenly alert. James did his best not to look at Carrow, knowing the cost an accurate solution would mean to the man.

"I will read to you the relevant portion of the solution: 'The person once known as Rose Bellamy is alive and well, happily married, gainfully employed, and beloved by many.'"

For a long moment, nobody spoke.

"Is that it?" Martha finally asked.

"No," said Mr. Trevelyan. "But the letter writer goes on to say that there is nothing in Rupert Bellamy's will that requires me to share the solution. In fact, she makes an argument for secrecy, beginning with an account of what she believes her grandfather would have wished, and ending with some statements that might be considered to skate rather perilously close to extortion by less charitably inclined minds."

Her grandfather—that meant the solution had come from Lilah. As he turned to her, she glanced up from her magazine.

"What manner of extortion did you use to make Mr. Trevelyan keep quiet?" Leo asked her, sounding amused, of all things.

"That's for me to know and you never to find out."

"I don't understand," Martha said.

"You don't need to, Aunt Martha," said Lilah. "Your cousin is well."

"But where is she? Camilla, surely you must want to know," Martha said.

"I've always said that Rose must have had her reasons and that it was none of my business," Camilla said, but James didn't think it was his imagination that the way she said this was much more brittle than it had been that first day.

213

"James?" Martha asked.

"I'm inclined to respect Mr. Trevelyan's point of view," James said.

Martha looked—there was no other word for it—defeated. "That's it, then, I suppose." Turning to the Carrows, who still stood near the door, she said, "I beg your pardon. We've taken up so much of your time. Have a lovely afternoon, my dears."

"I wonder how Trevelyan verified Lilah's solution," Leo murmured.

"Maybe he didn't," James said. "Maybe he just wanted Lilah to inherit the house."

Leo's eyebrows shot up, but he didn't disagree.

"Can I speak to you for a moment?" asked Lilah after Martha, Camilla, and the solicitor had left the room.

"Of course," said James.

"Privately." She glanced at Leo.

"I'll bring your luggage out to the car," offered Leo, and shut the door as he left the drawing room.

Lilah seemed reluctant to speak, instead examining the room as if she had never seen it. Well, maybe it seemed different to her now that it was her own.

"What will you do with it?" James asked.

"If you mean the house, other than making sure that Martha is comfortable here, I don't much care," she said. "But if you're talking about the money, it belongs to Will Carrow, doesn't it? My father stole what was in that box. It seems only right to pay Carrow back."

James wasn't so sure that Carrow would take the money, but figured that was for Lilah to sort out. "How did you know?"

"About Carrow? Remember, I spent the winter shifting between Viola and Cesario. Maybe I've just got used to looking at a face without thinking much about the gender of who the face belongs to." She shrugged. "Maybe I've spent years comparing my own reflection to the Bellamys and wondering at the difference. Or maybe I've always supposed that Rose Bellamy ran away and it wasn't hard for me to figure out why." She shrugged. "Or maybe it was a lucky guess."

James nodded. "You really won't tell your mother the truth about Carrow?"

"I'm good at keeping secrets from my mother." She looked pointedly at James. "And she's good at keeping secrets from me."

"She cares about you," James said, knowing how feeble this must sound. "You must know that the reason she let you take up acting was that she didn't want you to run away. She had already lost someone who ran away when they didn't get what they needed, and she wasn't going to let that happen again. Now, what did you want to speak to me about?"

"Would my father have lived if he had got his digitalis sooner?"

"Doubtful," James said. "In my experience, when a heart attack comes on that quickly, there's nothing to be done." This never stopped him, or most doctors, from trying everything in their repertoire.

Usually, families found this information comforting. When someone died suddenly, their families often wanted to pin-point exactly what went wrong, wanted to identify that one moment when things could have gone differently. Hearing that there wasn't such a moment often gave families some peace.

But what passed over Lilah's face wasn't peace. It wasn't anything at all. She was schooling her expression into one of cool neutrality, he realized. There was no reason for that, though.

Unless. He remembered what Camilla had said not a quarter of an hour ago, about believing her husband to have as good as murdered her sister. "Did you and your mother ever find your father's digitalis?" he asked gently.

She shook her head. "Of course not," and left the room.

He was left alone in the drawing room, dumbfounded and unsure of whether Lilah had just confessed to attempted murder. But, no, it wouldn't have been Lilah. He remembered Camilla insisting that she, not Lilah, would run upstairs to find the digitalis. She had been up there for what felt like ages. Had she simply decided that her husband wasn't worth saving?

And all that while, James had been downstairs, trying to save the man. It wasn't his place to decide who lived and who died. And in this instance, it certainly wasn't his business to decide who was culpable. The man would have died one way or the other, and whether a person had done wrong by merely intending another person to die was a question he'd leave to philosophers.

As for James, he would go home.

CHAPTER THIRTY-ONE

L eo supposed he could leave well enough alone. The mystery he had determined to solve for James's sake was now answered. There were loose ends, but they were of no importance to him, and likely hadn't even occurred to James, and so Leo ought to leave them be.

But Leo wasn't very good at leaving things be.

He thought about the cup of tea in Rupert Bellamy's room, the comfortable chair by his bed. He thought, too, of the way Martha said "Aunt Charlotte" but simply "Rupert."

And he realized what he should have understood as soon as he set foot in the house: Martha Dauntsey was grieving. Not two weeks earlier, she had lost the man with whom she had lived her entire adult life, and twenty of those years had been spent effectively alone with him. Leo didn't know if what had existed between them was friendship or something different, and he didn't think it mattered.

So when Lilah and James were closeted in the drawing room, Leo followed Martha into the kitchen. "I wonder if I can speak to you for a moment," he said as gently as he could.

She sat at the kitchen table, weariness in her every limb. "Do your worst, Mr. Page."

"Before I came here," Leo said, putting the kettle on the hob and taking a clean cup off the drying rack, "two women of Rupert Bellamy's generation said that he was too stolid a personality to go in for anything as theatrical as assembling his family for a reading of the will. And if they were correct, he certainly wouldn't have countenanced anything like the scavenger hunt we participated in this weekend."

"People change," said Martha unconvincingly.

"Perhaps," said Leo. "But I'm going to suggest another explanation. Perhaps someone else—an interested party, let's say—decided that they needed to know what happened twenty years ago. Perhaps they blamed themselves for what happened and, now that they were alone, weren't certain that they could face the rest of their own life without having that mystery put to rest. In that case, perhaps they took the liberty of rewriting certain portions of Rupert Bellamy's will and substituting a challenge that would encourage the truth to come out."

"That would be grievously unethical," said Martha.

"I'm no expert on ethics," said Leo. "I'm not interested in it in the least. What I do know is that a good number of things went wrong that summer twenty years ago, and if I were in the shoes of this interested party, I might want to know the extent to which my hands were dirty."

"She ran away."

"It might be better to think of it as starting a new life. A better life."

"You make it sound like a good thing. Like something brave."

"Yes. Definitely that." He wouldn't tell this woman that it wasn't her fault. But he could maybe give her peace that this story had a happy ending.

"How did you know about the will?"

"I found the will from which you borrowed the signature page. But moreover, the fake will did you harm. All the previous wills left you something substantial. It seemed impossible that in his dying days, Rupert Bellamy decided to do you out of a living."

"I wanted to know more than I wanted the house." Unspoken was that now she didn't know, nor did she have the house. "I daresay Lilah will let me stay on here."

"Lilah will insist, and we both know it. I don't think she would have said anything to Mr. Trevelyan if the house hadn't been at stake. Are you going to tell her? I'm afraid that if you don't, she's going to think that Gladys Button is her mother."

Martha looked up sharply at him. "Why on earth would she think that?"

"She was looking very closely at some pictures in the newspaper, and Gladys was small and fair. That's why she came here this weekend, I think. It was only natural to suppose that there might be some revelation in her grandfather's will, especially since he insisted on the beneficiaries gathering together. She was disappointed."

"Camilla and I will need to talk." There was a dread underlying her words, and Leo realized that for all that had happened in the past two days, Camilla and Martha would still rather do anything than discuss the unpleasant.

"I have one other question and then I'll let you be. Why did you leave James that photograph of his father?"

"I had to make sure the will left him something or it would have looked odd."

Leo wanted there to be a reason for James to have been brought back into the reach of these people and this house. He wanted to hear that Martha meant to atone for years of

219

ignoring her cousin, or even that she had intended the gesture to be cruel. He would have been satisfied to know that she simply thought James would have wanted the photograph.

Leo didn't get angry terribly often; it was dangerous, in his business, to have a short fuse. But the idea that there hadn't been any reason at all made him close to furious. He couldn't stand that James had been used, that his feelings had been treated as unimportant now as they had been twenty years earlier.

Footsteps sounded in the hallway leading to the kitchen, and Leo turned to see James.

"How long will it take to get back to Wychcomb St. Mary?" James asked after they had taken their leave of Martha.

"The way I mean to drive? Three hours. There's only one thing left for me to do. I'm going to pretend I left something upstairs. But I'm going to sneak into your uncle's room and commit a tiny little felony."

"If you're going back to steal the picture of me as a gangly twelve-year-old, you needn't go to the trouble. I already took it." He reached into his coat pocket and withdrew a photograph.

Leo stared at him. "Am I that obvious? How lowering."

"Every time you come across a photograph of me in one of Cora's books, you ask her for it. If you were trying to be subtle, you should work on your impressions."

Leo took the photograph, gave it another glance, and carefully placed it in his jacket pocket. "I like tangible evidence that I didn't conjure you up," he said. "Now let's go home."

CHAPTER THIRTY-TWO

I n the end, it was James who drove home, and they were hardly out of Cornwall before Leo fell asleep in the passenger seat. Leo slept so deeply he didn't even stir when James drove over a particularly potholed stretch of road, only waking when James pulled the car to a stop in front of his house in Wychcomb St. Mary.

"Come on," James said softly, nudging Leo in the shoulder. "Get up and you can finish your nap in a proper bed."

Leo muttered something incoherent but got out and went around to the back of the car to help James unload their baggage.

James fiddled with his latch key and pushed open the door to the house. The smell of the place—the lemon soap the cleaner used on the furniture, mingled with a bit of disinfectant wafting over from the surgery—was something he never quite noticed when he was home, but after a few days away, it was both obvious and soothing.

He hung his coat and hat on the hooks where he always hung them. It was hard to believe he had only been away for a little over two days, and peculiar to realize that two days was all it took for his own home to feel slightly off kilter but also a blessed relief. He ran his finger along the table where he habitually tossed his keys. It was probably just exhaustion and stress catching up with him, but that stupid table felt impossibly dear, almost miraculous in its familiarity.

"I don't ever want to leave again," he said.

"Neither do I," said Leo, dropping James's suitcase to the hall floor.

If it hadn't been for the dead seriousness of Leo's tone, James might have thought it a mere glib line. Instead, he turned to face the man. "What does that mean?"

It wasn't often that Leo looked flustered. Hell, it wasn't often that Leo looked anything other than completely competent and in control. But now he scuffed the toe of his shoe against the floor like a bashful schoolboy. "This last job was—" He broke off, shaking his head.

"Worse than usual?" James suggested. He had guessed as much, given the state Leo was in when he returned from his trip—weary and somehow brittle. What he hadn't expected was for Leo to want to talk about it.

"No," Leo said. "That's exactly it. It wasn't any different than any other job. It's me that's different."

Since Christmas, Leo had been saying that he wanted to quit, and James had very carefully avoided saying anything that Leo might take as pressure. It was Leo's decision, and not James's business. And yet, maybe it was James's business to support Leo in doing what he had already made up his mind to do. James had said he wanted a life with Leo. Maybe he needed to act like it.

"Are they putting pressure on you to keep working?" James asked.

"No, thank God," Leo said.

"Quit, then. You can quit tomorrow. You don't need the money."

"Like hell I don't."

"Let's get something to eat," James said, and put a hand on the small of Leo's back to lead him to the kitchen. He ran the sink for a moment to clear any stale water from the pipes, then filled the kettle. While the kettle was heating on the hob, he turned to face Leo. "You have a home. You have food. You don't have to risk your life and safety unless that's what you want to do."

"I've been doing this in one way or another for my entire adult life, not to mention the bit before that. I don't know what else I'd do. I'm certainly not qualified for anything else. I don't have any way of earning my keep." He rubbed the back of his neck. "I'm twenty-nine."

The last time James asked, Leo had been twenty-eight, and he didn't know if that meant Leo had had a birthday since then or if he didn't know his own damned age, and either explanation made James want to cry. Or possibly bake Leo a cake. Or both. "That means you have plenty of time to figure out what you want to do with the next few decades," James said. "If that's what you choose."

"Christ, stop being so decent, James."

"If you quit, I don't want it to be because of me."

"But it will be! Don't you see? You've made me totally unfit for that life. I can't go around putting bullets in people when you look at me like—fuck, like I'm something special. And I can't very well let other people put bullets in me when all the while I know how you'd feel about that. I'm just developing a strong anti-bullet stance all around, it seems."

The kettle began to hiss and James took out two cups and

a pair of tea bags, then poured the water, conscious that his hands were far from steady. "I'm not sure whether to apologize," he said, his back to Leo. "No, scratch that. You are something special and I'm not going to apologize for letting you know that I think so. And as for you being hurt—well, I imagine you'd feel the same about me being hurt."

"You know I would," Leo said, coming up behind him. "The trouble is that I love you," he said. "And it's ruined me for gainful employment."

James turned around. "Bugger gainful employment." And he kissed Leo, trying not to be too frantic about it, one hand on Leo's jaw and the other hard on his hip. "I love you too."

"I can't just follow you about like a lost lamb," Leo said. "I have to do something."

James was tempted to say that of course Leo could follow him like a lost lamb; he could lie about and do nothing but take up space and James wouldn't even begin to mind. But that wasn't what Leo needed to hear. "And so you will. You don't need to know what that is quite yet."

"I can't just stay with you."

Now, this James couldn't pretend to hear with equanimity. "This is your home," he said firmly, stroking Leo's cheekbone with a thumb. "Isn't it?" He tried not to sound as if he desperately needed to hear Leo agree.

Leo sighed, but not without one corner of his mouth twitching upwards. "You know it is."

"Then you'll treat it that way, if I have anything to say about it. If you're worried about what people will think, we've already put it about that you're my lodger. So, now you're my unemployed lodger. How is that any different? Nobody's going to jump to the conclusion that you're my...my kept man, or whatever it is you're afraid of."

That, at least, made Leo laugh a little. "I have some money saved. Precious few opportunities to spend much these past few years. Besides, I'm not nearly pretty enough to be anyone's kept man."

"Don't sell yourself short," James said.

"I don't want to take anything from you. It's too unfair if in addition to putting up with me, you're also housing me. And don't say you aren't putting up with me. Who and what I am requires a certain amount of moral contortionism for you. When you look at me on the pillow next to yours, you must realize that."

James smoothed the hair off Leo's forehead and looked him in the eye. "Yes," he said, fighting the urge to brush aside Leo's worry. Everything Leo said was true, although not as dramatic as Leo made it out to be. "If you'll excuse the tautology, if you weren't who and what you are, then your head wouldn't be on that pillow next to mine."

"But—"

"No, let me finish. You keep saying things like 'who you are' and 'what you do,' as if I don't want to be reminded of the truth. So let's stop speaking in euphemisms. You lied and cheated and hurt and killed for a long time, generally for a good cause, but perhaps not always. And maybe it doesn't matter how good the cause is, maybe those things are always wrong. I don't know. What I do know is that I love you, every last dangerous and dishonest inch of you, and I wouldn't have it any other way." Leo shook his head and looked ready to argue, so James kissed him, and then kissed him some more. "I promise to keep telling you that," James whispered. "Let me do that, all right?"

"Yeah," Leo said, speaking the words into the wool of James's jumper. "I still feel like I'm a bad bargain."

"Leo. I feel like I'm a bad bargain too. I think that's just how love works. Well, for neurotic people, at least. Sometimes you look at me like I'm marvelous and I think you must not have realized I'm a ball of nerves, and that's on a good day."

And now Leo was kissing him, backing him up hard against the sink and digging his fingers into James's back.

"We should drink our tea before it steeps too long," James said, being very sensible, he thought. Leo responded by raising an eyebrow and dropping to his knees.

"Go ahead and drink your tea," Leo said, his words muffled by the fabric of James's trousers. "I'm busy."

And, well, James couldn't really argue with that. He tangled his fingers in Leo's hair.

CHAPTER THIRTY-THREE

L eo wondered when James's mattress became the standard against which all other mattresses were to be judged. Objectively, it was a bit lumpy and sagged in the middle, but it felt correct in a way that rendered other mattresses unpleasantly alien.

Long ago, Leo had become used to waking up in strange places. But now when he woke up anywhere that wasn't James's bed, he was aware of disappointment before he was even awake enough to form coherent thought.

He was going to stay, this time for good. Eventually this mattress would be his mattress too, and maybe he'd stop feeling vaguely fraudulent when thinking of this house as home.

"I have to go to London," he groaned.

"Good morning to you, too," James said from beside him. "Do you have to go right this minute?"

It was Monday morning. He really ought to go today. The powers that be were not going to be pleased that he had bunked on his debrief. "Tomorrow. To give notice."

"Do spies give notice? How very ordinary."

"I suppose we're about to find out."

"There's something that's been bothering me," James said. "I

227

understand why Camilla adopted Lilah—she and Martha had just lost someone and might not want to see the baby go to strangers. But why did Sir Anthony agree to raise Lilah as his own? He doesn't strike me as the sort of man to do that."

Leo rolled over onto his side to face James. "I wonder if he thought he was buying Camilla's silence. Or maybe he just felt guilty. I think he did care about Camilla, at least at first."

"Should we have told Lilah what we learned?"

"You're asking *me* an ethical question?"

"Why shouldn't I?"

Leo gave James a look that he hoped conveyed exactly what he thought of that sentiment. "In that case, I think it depends on whether you want anything more to do with them. If you don't, then it's not your business. You can leave them to sort out their own secrets. But if you plan to have a relationship with any of them, especially Lilah, I don't think you can keep that from her."

"I like Lilah," James said. "It might be nice to have one blood relation I keep in touch with."

"Not Camilla and Martha?"

"I'm sure I'll send Christmas cards," James said, with more asperity in his voice than Leo was used to hearing there. "I'm glad I saw them, but I'm afraid I don't feel very kindly about them having, well, abandoned me, not to put too fine a point on it. I already have a family and it's not them." Then he frowned. "Leo, do I hear chickens in the garden?"

After they sat down to eat some scrambled eggs, Leo unwrapped the canvas he had bought from Mrs. Carrow. It was an oil painting of a rocky stretch of coastline, a lighthouse barely visible in the distance. It was not one of the pretty watercolors that she sold to tourists, but was instead bleak and unforgiving. It was also, she had told him, a part of the coast that she saw every day when she took a walk.

James stood by Leo's side and studied the painting. "Why this one?" he finally asked.

Leo swallowed, hoping he could find the words to explain. "She has a way of painting that shows the unvarnished truth. You can see that she knows this place—every craggy rock, every straggly weed. She sees it for what it is, and she doesn't need to dress it up." Leo was sure he was making a hash of this, but then James nodded.

"The scales have dropped from her eyes, but in a way that doesn't stop her from loving what she sees," James said.

"Yes," Leo said in relief. "Exactly that." And when he reached out, James's hand was already there, waiting for him.

That afternoon they stopped by Little Briars and presented the two ladies with the bare facts of the case.

"What bothers me," said Cora, idly winding a ball of wool, "is why Gladys ran away."

"Because the police arrived, of course," said Edith. "She would have been worried that with her past, she would be blamed for whatever had happened to Rose."

"I meant why did she run off on Saturday night? That morning she told someone on the telephone that she had 'given him until tonight' or something to that effect." She looked at Leo. "You see that your Mrs. Mudge was quite right that she had precisely the sort of head that one can fill with bad ideas. I'd wager she never thought of blackmailing anyone until she fell in with that man."

"What man?" James asked.

"The man on the phone, of course," Cora said. "Possibly a woman, but most likely a man."

"It so often is," agreed Edith.

"Too right. In any event, from that telephone call, I can only suppose that Gladys had given Marchand a deadline for paying her. Why run off before she got her money?"

"Perhaps he told her he wasn't paying," suggested James.

"I'd have hardly thought Sir Anthony Marchand was the 'publish and be damned' sort," said Edith. "For goodness' sake, give me that yarn before you tangle it all up, Cora." Edith snatched the wool away.

"Camilla recognized her at dinner," said Leo. "She put on her spectacles to examine a photograph James showed her, and she glanced around the table. A few minutes later, when they were discussing the former servants, she said 'Gladys Button!' and looked directly at her." Leo saw that James was giving him a highly reproachful look. "We had other things to think about! It didn't seem important."

"Ah. The poor girl thought it was a threat," said Cora.

"The poor girl was nearly forty," pointed out Edith.

"And then there was the business with the wine glasses," said Cora. "If you, James, wondered whether the spill had been engineered to slip something into Gladys's drink, then you can be sure that Gladys had the same idea."

The implication, Leo realized, was that James was as unsuspecting as a baby. He smiled into his tea.

"Between Camilla recognizing her and Sir Anthony evidently trying to poison her," Cora went on, "Gladys must have decided that Anthony Marchand's money was more trouble than it was worth."

"I rang the Cornwall constabulary this morning," said Leo. "There was nothing in those glasses. And nothing in Marchand's system, either, except for a very small amount of

Seconal, consistent with a standard dose."

"You just rang them up," James said, looking long-suffering. "And demanded a toxicology report."

"I may have called in a few favors." He was going to have to send a lavish flower arrangement to Mrs. Patel. Or possibly a set of throwing knives.

"So he died of a simple heart attack," James said. "That's a relief. But then what happened to Camilla's medicine?" Leo watched as the penny dropped. "Sir Anthony took it himself?"

"He was anxious about being blackmailed," Leo said. "Anyone would be."

"But he didn't tell his wife because he was a giant hypocrite," James grumbled.

"I daresay he was in quite a state after receiving that blackmail letter," Edith said. "And then his blackmailer disappears before he can pay up. No wonder he had a heart attack when he heard Gladys had left."

"I wonder if the henna will wash out of her hair," mused Cora. "I had to henna my hair once"—she turned to Leo and James—"I needed a quick change of appearance after a job went wrong."

Edith made a harrumphing sound. "The ambassador! What a swine."

"It took ages for the henna to wash out. I wound up cutting it all off."

"And very dashing it was, my dear."

James leaned forward and poured fresh tea into everyone's cups.

Maybe it could be as simple as this. Maybe a retired spy could think about jobs gone wrong in terms of the unfortunate hair colors one was forced to adopt. Maybe Leo could be a good person without understanding whether he used to be a bad person, and maybe he didn't even have to think about any of that right now.

"I think we should go to the seaside this summer," James said as they walked home. "Maybe for a fortnight? Not anywhere near Blackthorn, of course, but perhaps Lyme Regis? Or maybe Weymouth. Just for a little holiday."

"A holiday," Leo repeated.

"Well, yes. If the idea appeals to you, that is."

Leo imagined ice creams and walks on the beach and bathing trunks. James would freckle and his shoulders would turn pink in the sun. He would make friends with every old lady in the hotel and pet every dog on the beach.

And sometimes James would look at him the way he was doing right now, with affection and an easy possessive confidence, as if he knew how much Leo adored him but wasn't going to make too big a fuss about it.

"A holiday," Leo repeated again, like he was trying the word out, trying it on for size.

He had taken holidays, he supposed. There were times between jobs when there was nowhere to report and he had been at loose ends, so he had time to see sights or lounge about. Sometimes there were even people to spend that free time with—colleagues on leave, locals who didn't know any better—and that had been fine. None of those had been—premeditated holidays, he supposed.

But this—planning a holiday six months in advance, packing suitcases filled with holiday things and probably much less weaponry than usual—that would be new. Going on a holiday with someone because they were the person you went on holidays with and ate supper with and cleaned your teeth beside—that would be new as well.

"If you want," James said, so casually, as if he didn't know Leo was standing a few inches away from him slowly losing his mind.

Yes, Leo wanted that. He wanted to see James on a beach with his hair ruined by the wind. He wanted to sit on the sand and eat packed sandwiches and throw crusts to the birds that circled overhead. He wanted a span of empty time filled with nothing but James and bright yellow sunshine.

He cleared his throat and tried to say that yes, he would go on holiday with James, he would go on as many holidays as James saw fit to take, for as long as he was invited. All that came out was "yes."

"And then when we get back, we can buy a new sofa," James said.

"What?" Leo wasn't certain how they had got from the seashore to sofas.

"Our sofa is too small for both of us to fit on comfortably."

It was true. If one of them tried to stretch out, somebody's feet were always under the other's thighs or on their lap. And if they both wanted to lie down, it was a shambles—they had to be on top of one another, Leo's face tucked into the heat of James's neck.

"I like the sofa," Leo said. "I like how it is."

"I do too. I just thought—"

"If we get another, we should get one just the same size."

"Then that's exactly what we'll do."

Every *we*, every *our* sounded like percussive notes, like a bell ringing out the unlikely truth of the words, and Leo wanted to keep saying them again and again.

Preview of Tommy Cabot Was Here

TOMMY CABOT WAS ♡ HERE

a romance

CAT SEBASTIAN

Massachusetts, 1959

Surely by now, after a full month at Greenfield, Everett ought to have gotten over the dizzying sense of unreality he experienced whenever he remembered that he wasn't one of the uniform-clad students. Here it was, already October, the leaves red and orange with the passing of time, not a trace of summer left in the air, and he still couldn't shake the idea that the past twenty years amounted to nothing more than a daydream, and that the next time he walked into his classroom he would need to sit at one of the desks rather than stand before the chalkboard.

The great lawn was filled with parents who had come for the annual exercise in staged reassurance known as Visiting Sunday, during which they could see for themselves that their sons hadn't wasted away or returned to a state of nature after a month out of their care. Everett half expected to look up and see his own parents in their shabby old-fashioned clothes, instead of these strangers—some of whom, astonishingly, were younger than himself. The children had been combed and scrubbed and stuffed into their Sunday clothes by housemistresses, faculty wives, and in the case of one exceptionally bedraggled young man, Everett himself. That too—the taming of the cowlick, the unpicking of shoelaces, the last-minute sewing on of mismatched buttons—had sent Everett's mind careening wildly backward to a time when he had performed the same tasks for his classmates.

He shook hands with a few of his students' parents, made the appropriate remarks, and had a cigarette halfway to his lips when he saw—well, he was ashamed to admit, even to himself, that his first thought was that he was seeing a ghost. But ghosts surely did not take surreptitious bites of chocolate bars, nor could they possibly have leaves clinging to the backs of their trousers from illicit leaps into the gardeners' neatly raked leaf piles. But if not a ghost, then who was this child with his black hair and blue eyes, that unmistakable Cabot nose, and that even more unmistakable Cabot air of pedigreed good humor?

Well, Greenfield had to be crawling with Cabots, surely. It stood to reason that the Cabot family would as a matter of course send its sons to the school that had educated its fathers and grandfathers and which boasted not only the Cabot Library but also the Cabot Gymnasium and Cabot Tennis Courts. This child, who had just shoved the entire chocolate bar into his mouth and stuck the wrapper up his sleeve before turning to the headmaster with the insouciance of a born sinner, could be any one of a number of Cabot progeny.

As Everett watched, a man approached the child, casually passed him a handkerchief, and stuck out his hand to greet the approaching headmaster. With a shaky hand, Everett managed to light his cigarette. He inhaled and did the math: Tommy's son was born in '47 and would now be twelve, so just the right age for first form. Everett let his gaze slide up the man who stood beside the child, up the legs of a suit that probably cost more than Everett's car, up the lean body he had spent fifteen years trying not to think about, and finally to the face of the man who had been his ruin.

He puffed out a surprised gust of smoke. If not for the child and the math, he might not have recognized Tommy. The man was in desperate need of a haircut, and whatever efforts he had made with a razor must have happened in a dark room with a dull blade. Around his eyes were lines that hadn't been visible in the society photographs Everett's mother still insisted on

237

clipping out and sending to him. There was something in the way he held himself, a rigidity and tension, that was new and unsettling, and would have been disconcerting to see on any Cabot, but most of all Tommy.

Before Everett could quite make sense of the fact that Tommy Cabot was suddenly a few feet away, Tommy was turning toward him. Everett froze. He didn't do terribly well when things didn't go according to plan, and he certainly hadn't planned on suddenly coming face to face with Tommy. If he had been prepared, he would have come up with something to say, something safe and polite. But now he was faced with the decision of whether to seek cover in a nearby cluster of faculty or walk toward Tommy and the headmaster and probably make a mess of things. He stepped forward. No matter what had happened, he wasn't hiding from Tommy. He owed them both more than that.

"Mr. Clayton," Everett said to the headmaster, and then turned to Tommy, his hand outstretched in the best approximation of a polite greeting that he could manage.

Tommy's face split into a smile that made Everett's stomach drop. "Hell and—language, damn it, sorry about that Daniel," he said, ruffling the child's hair, "damnation, is that you, Ev? Of course it is, come here." And then his arms were around Everett, who was left holding the cigarette in one hand, the other hand patting stupidly at Tommy's back. He smelled the same, damn him, like the sort of aftershave you could only buy at a department store. And if he was broader and had lost all the angularity of youth, his body still felt recognizable, mapping onto Everett's body in the same way it always had. Everett extricated himself as soon Tommy loosened his hold.

"Of course," Mr. Clayton said. "You were in the same

graduating class."

"Class of 1941. We were roommates," Tommy supplied.

"In that case, I'll leave you to catching up," the headmaster said, and proceeded across the lawn to shake hands with more parents. Everett wanted to call him back. Or follow him. Or possibly sink into the earth.

"What are you doing here?" Tommy asked. He was still smiling, as if this was excellent, such a happy coincidence, what a delightful reunion. "Last I heard you were in England."

"I only came back a few months ago." Everett's voice sounded rusty and strange, as if he hadn't used it in the years since last seeing Tommy. He was afraid that if he spoke, all that would come out would be a confession, fifteen years' worth of *I miss you*. Instead he took a drag from his cigarette and tried to school his expression into professional nonchalance.

"This is Daniel's first year," Tommy said, gesturing at the spot where his son had stood a minute earlier. "What year is your son in?"

Everett gritted his teeth at the reminder that of course Tommy would assume that Everett had made the same choices Tommy had, that after all these years Tommy still didn't realize that not everybody sailed through life without consequence. "I don't—I'm not," he stammered. "I'm teaching here."

"You aren't one of Daniel's teachers, are you?"

"I only teach sixth and seventh years," Everett said. "I haven't seen Patricia." That was the ticket, remind himself—remind *both* of them—that Tommy was married. He pointedly gazed around the lawn for a bright blond head.

"Oh," Tommy said after a moment. "She isn't here. She's in California."

Everett frowned. California was about as far as a person

239

could get from a husband whose life was divided between Boston and Washington. "Well," he said tightly. "Give her my best." He had liked Patricia. Hell and damn, he had been there on their wedding day. He had danced with her while she kept up a steady stream of chatter that even at the age of twenty-three Everett understood to be the sort of kindness meant to save him from having to make conversation. Now he wondered if she had known, if she had suspected the special kind of hell it was for him to be Tommy's best man.

Tommy pressed his lips together. "I'll be sure to do that," he said. He had gray at his temples. His shirt was badly ironed and his tie had only a perfunctory knot. That last detail was horribly familiar—God only knew how many times Everett had tugged Tommy behind the chapel or into a stairwell and insisted on making sense of his tie. Now he was old enough to understand that Cabots could get away with sloppiness. He also understood that letting Everett fuss over him had been part of Tommy's game. He had let Everett have those proprietary touches, had let Everett believe that whatever existed between them actually mattered. Tommy was a Cabot, born with a silver spoon and the unchallenged conviction that he could have whatever he wanted; back then, he had wanted Everett, and hadn't ever stopped to consider what harm he might be doing.

"I see a parent I ought to speak to," Everett lied, and left Tommy standing alone.

* * *

Tommy needed a drink. He also needed a nap, and possibly to lie down on that hideous carpet in his living room and stare at the ceiling and cry. Nobody had told him how much of his late thirties would involve lying on floors and crying.

He watched Everett stalk across the lawn. The man looked exactly the same as he had the last time they had seen one another. His battered wire-framed glasses had been swapped out for a heavy black pair, but they sat crookedly on his nose the way they always had. His pale brown hair had been combed into submission and neatly parted on the side, but Tommy knew that all it would take was a stiff wind to reveal its curls. Everett still had the same air of brittle rigidity, as if his collar had been starched three times over. But now it was as if that starch had been baked into his bones. Tommy had used to love coaxing Everett out of his stuffier moods, teasing and cajoling until Everett finally gave in and laughed. The man he saw now looked like he hadn't smiled, let alone laughed, in years.

But Everett still had the same smattering of freckles on his nose, and that too made Tommy want to cry. To be fair, everything made him want to cry these days. That, he supposed, was what came of resolutely refusing to experience human emotions for the better part of a decade. They wound up making a huge mess when they finally did come out, like a suppressed sneeze.

Tommy still found it hard to accept how thoroughly Everett had walked away from him fifteen years ago. It had taken five unanswered letters for Tommy to get the picture that Everett didn't want to hear from him. He had even asked a mutual friend whether there was something wrong with postal service in Oxford, and in response got a peculiar look and the intelligence that Everett was writing to people, just not, it would seem, to Tommy. It made no sense at the time. Everett had been his best man, much to the confusion of his

241

brothers. Everett had been rock-solid during the ceremony, remembering everything from the rings to all the names of Tommy's aunts. And then he and Pat came back from their honeymoon and discovered that Everett had put an ocean between them, without so much as a word.

That had been his first real loss. He had lost friends in the war, but that was the first time he had wanted to draw the curtains and grieve. He had asked Pat—not once, not twice, but almost daily for months—if he had done or said something unforgivable the day of the wedding. But then his oldest brother had won a seat in Congress, and Daniel had been born, and suddenly his days were busy, if not exactly complete. He had thought that would be enough, and for a while it almost was.

Seeing Everett today was just another reminder of how far Tommy had fallen, of how little was left of the man he had wanted to be. Fifteen years ago, Tommy had a bright future and a loving family; now he was alone and unmoored.

He crossed the lawn to say goodbye to Daniel, who was with a few of the younger children, all of whom looked like they were about twenty minutes away from becoming feral. He went to shake Daniel's hand, but Daniel pulled him into a hug. "It'll be all right, Dad," he whispered. Tommy managed something about seeing him the following weekend and congratulated himself on not weeping all over his son's shoulder in front of the kid's classmates.

As he made his way toward the road that led into town, he saw Everett clustered with a group of parents. His back was straight; his hair still hadn't gotten mussed. Fifteen years was a long time, and maybe there wasn't much left of the Everett he had loved. Maybe that had all been in Tommy's head in the first place. Mere boyish antics. Experimentation, as his psychoanalyst had suggested. Maybe Tommy had driven Everett away by being too—too bent, too effusive, too selfish, too much.

He shoved his hands in his pockets, which would probably ruin his suit, but it wasn't like he had much use for hand-sewn suits anymore. He made his way down the road, and when he finally looked over his shoulder, the peaks and towers of Greenfield had disappeared into the autumn foliage.

Tommy Cabot Was Here is available just about everywhere.

About the Author

Cat Sebastian writes queer historical romance. She lives in a swampy part of the South but also on twitter.

For information about all Cat's books, please visit her website, CatSebastian.com.

You can connect with me on:
- 🐦 http://twitter.com/catswrites
- ✎ https://www.instagram.com/catswrites